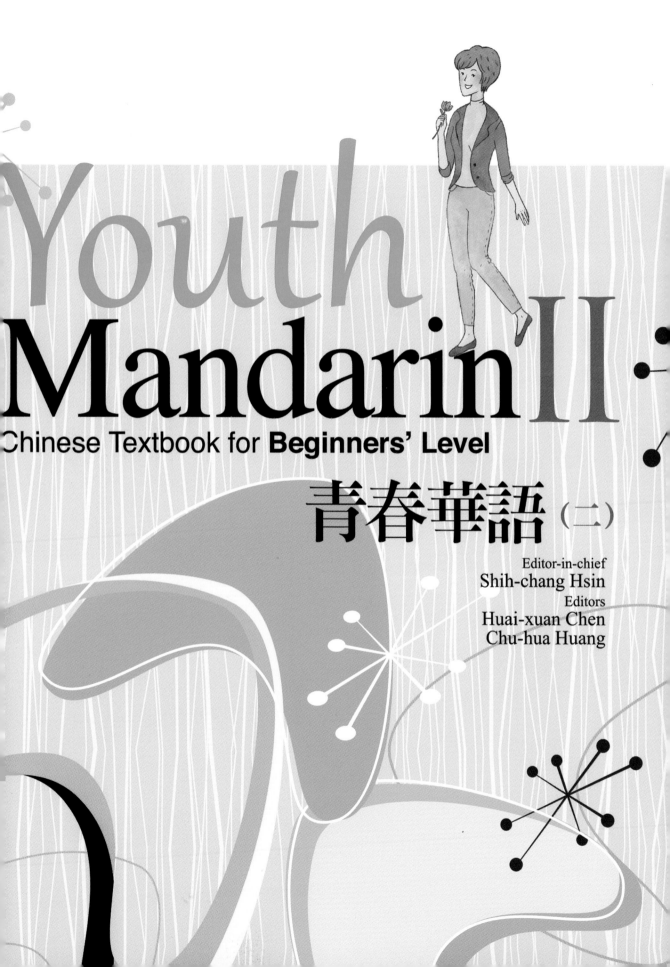

Youth Mandarin II

Chinese Textbook for **Beginners' Level**

青春華語 (二)

Editor-in-chief
Shih-chang Hsin
Editors
Huai-xuan Chen
Chu-hua Huang

Preface

A. Introducing the Book

1. Target readers: beginners in senior high school or junior high school.
2. Duration: one semester, suitable for the schools with less Chinese learning hours.
3. The texts come in both traditional and simplified Chinese. Pinyin is also included. A glossary is attached at the end of the book.
4. Chinese characters: 768 different Chinese characters are included.
5. Vocabulary: 472 words (meaning units) are included.
6. Sentence patterns: 59 sentence patterns are included.

B. Structure and Concepts

There are 12 units in this book and each unit starts with warm-up activities to engage the students. Following are the three major sections of a unit: core activities, after-class practice and exercise, and supplementary materials.

1. Core Activities

There are two lessons in one unit. Each lesson includes a story, a dialogue, discussions, vocabulary, expressions, and grammar.

  a. Story: the story is written in English so as to help the learner understand the context of the dialogue that follows.
  b. Dialogue: readers can learn different speech styles from the characters for their backgrounds, genders, and personalities differ.
  c. Discussions: discussions help students understand the content and meaning of the dialogue.
  d. Vocabulary and expressions: new words are those that show up in

the book for the first time and expressions are set phrases such as: 怎麼了? and 太棒了! We put vocabulary and expressions into separate sheets so the teachers can apply different teaching methods when leading practice sessions.

e. Grammar: emphasizing on sentence patterns; useful sentence patterns are provided.

2. After-class Practice and Exercise

After-class practice and exercise come after core activities and consist of grammar practice and application.

a. Practice: have the students repeatedly practice sentence structures until they become innate.

b. Exercise: applying what has been learned by completing a dialogue in the given scenario or completing related tasks.

3. Supplementary Materials

Supplementary explanation and culture note are provided at the end of every unit.

a. Supplementary explanation: explaining some language nuances that need to be paid attention to or listing out some supplementary words.

b. Culture note: notes on sceneries and historical sites, festivals and customs, taboos, dining culture, and etc. are provided in accordance with the topic of each unit.

The textbook is developed by the Videoconferencing Chinese Team (VC Chinese). VC Chinese is a research team formed by professors and graduate assistants for instructional materials development and teacher training for distance Chinese teaching.

——VC Chinese Team

編輯前言

A. 教材簡介

1.使用對象：本教材是針對高中與初中年齡層的華語學習者所編寫。

2.教學時間：可使用一個學期，適於每週中文課時數較少的學校使用。

3.課文均有繁體字、簡體字及漢語拼音。課本最後附有全冊的生詞表。

4.漢字量：本教材共有768不同的漢字。

5.生詞量：本教材共有472個生詞。

6.句型量：本教材共有59個中文句型。

B. 教材結構及編寫理念

本教材共有12個單元（Unit），每個單元首先以暖身活動引起學習動機。再分為三大部分：教學核心活動、課後練習活動、課外補充材料。

1.教學核心活動

各單元之下有兩課：每課包括故事情節、對話、討論、生詞、固定說法及語法，此為教學核心部分。

a.故事情節：先以英文敘述故事情節，讓學習者進入真實情境，了解語言實際使用的場景。

b.對話：透過不同背景、性別、個性的人物展開對話，藉以顯現不同人物，語言使用的風格也有所不同，同時也是學習者學習模仿的語言形式。

c.討論：經過問題討論，確認學習者了解對話的內容及含意。

d.詞彙及固定說法：詞彙為學習者首次學習的詞彙，而固定說法則是一些常用習慣語，如：「怎麼了？」「太棒了！」，我們希望將這些習慣用語和生詞做切分，以便老師在練習時可採用不同練習方式。

e.語法：主要以句型為主，強調功能實用性。

2.課後練習活動

教學核心活動結束之後，進行課後練習，分為語法操練和應用練習。

a.語法操練（Practice）：以語法句型機械式操練為主，在於鞏固形式，強調熟練性。

b.應用練習（Exercise）：以完成情境對話及任務活動方式，真實運用所學。

3.課外補充材料

每單元結束後，提供與單元主題相關之語言及文化知識。

a.語言補充：說明一些語言形式使用注意事項，或補充相關詞彙。

b.文化知識：根據各單元主題，補充相關的文化知識，包括介紹風景名勝、節慶習俗、生活禁忌、餐飲習慣等。

——VC Chinese Team

Topics Functions & Language Skills

各單元主題功能和語言技能

UNIT	SUBJECT	TOPIC	LANGUAGE SKILL
UNIT1	How Was Your Winter Vacation?	Holiday Activities	Describing Scenery & Activities
UNIT2	Here's Something for You	Gift	Expression of Politeness & Courtesy
UNIT3	Happy New Year!	Festival	Describing Festivals & Folklore
UNIT4	What Are You Doing on New Year's Eve?	Event	Describing Emotions & Comforting
UNIT5	Do You Like Kung Fu Movies?	Movie	Invitation & Describing Movies
UNIT6	What Are You Interested In?	Interest	Introducing Your Interest
UNIT7	Let's Make Spring Rolls at My House	Chinese food	Describing Cooking Process
UNIT8	Go, Mark! Go!	Sports Event	Describing Sports Event
UNIT9	Do You Want to Apply for the Student Exchange Program?	Studying Abroad	Talking about Learning Plan
UNIT10	Let's Go to the Theme Park!	Theme Park	Introducing Teenagers Leisure Culture
UNIT11	The Exam Is Coming Up!	Examination	Comparison of Examination System
UNIT12	Life in High School	Student Life	Comparing Culture

Grammar & Cultural Notes
文法和文化點

Unit	Lesson	Grammar	Cultural Note
1	1	1. N. , V.+得怎麼樣？ 2. DirV+來/去 3. 更+adj	1. Yu Garden （豫園） 2. National Palace Museum （故宮博物院）
	2	1. V+到 2. 好像+adj 3. 不是…就是…	
2	1	1. 從+地方+動詞+來 2. 數詞+量詞+數詞+量詞 3. 名詞+比+名詞+形容詞+數詞+量詞	1. Chinese Gift-giving Etiquette （送禮的文化） 2. Twelve Chinese Zodiac Signs （十二生肖）
	2	1. 來+V 2. 是用+N+V+的 3. 形容詞重疊+的	
3	1	1. 跟…一樣 2. Verb+完+Noun，就+Verb	1. The Story of Nain （年獸的故事） 2. Chinese New Year Food and Customs （年菜跟習俗）
	2	1. Verb+在+地方 2. …，可是…	
4	1	1. 最後一+量+（N） 2. …好了 3. 還好…，…	1. Weiya – Year-end Dinner Party （尾牙） 2. New Year's Gala （新年晚會）
	2	1. 人+VOV得… 2. 輪到+人+V了	
5	1	1. A跟B約+時間／在地方 2. 人+對…有興趣	About Kung Fu （功夫）
	2	1. 怎麼那麼+adj 2. VOV了+時間 3. 人+來不及+V	
6	1	1. 不但…還… 2. A陪B+V	Euphemisms in Chinese （中國人的委婉藝術）
	2	1. 忙著+V 2. A、B什麼的 3. 有空的話，我想…	

Unit	Lesson	Grammar	Cultural Note
7	1	1. 把+N+V+RC(Resultative Complement) 2. 把+N+V+DC(Directional Complement)	1. Eight Regional Cuisines in China （中國最有名的八大菜系） 2. Chinese Dining Etiquette （華人吃飯的禮節）
	2	1. 看看+V了沒有/嗎？ 2. 這是+N+第+NU+次+V 3. 多+V+幾+NU+N	
8	1	1. 就要+V+了 2. 差一點就+V+了 3. 本來+V，後來+V+了。	Eastern and Western Attitudes Toward Sport （中西方對運動的看法差異）
	2	1. V+不下 2. 雖然…可是…	
9	1	1. 關於+…的問題，… 2. 每+量+N1的N2都不一樣	Introducing Taiwan （臺灣簡介）
	2	1. 不管A還是B，都… 2. 不管怎麼樣，人都…	
10	1	1. 為了… 2. Adj+死了 3. 趁…	Weekend Culture （休閒文化大不同）
	2	1. V+Time Spent+才+V+ 2. V+Time Spent就+	
11	1	1. …快要到了 2. V不／得C 3. 我以為…	Education System in Taiwan （臺灣的教育制度）
	2	1. 到…才+V 2. 寧可…也不要…	
12	1	1. 為了+目的，人+得+V 2. 幸好…，要不然…	Introducing Beijing （北京簡介）
	2	1. 同一+量+N 2. 這樣一來	

Abbreviation

詞性簡表

Abbreviation	Case	Chinese
Adv	Adverb	副詞
AV	Auxiliary Verb	助動詞
MW	Measure Word	量詞
N	Noun	名詞
NU	Number	數字
PW	Place Word	地方詞
P	Particle	助詞
QW	Question Word	疑問詞
Adj / SV	Adjective / Stative Verb	形容詞 / 狀態動詞
TW	Time Word	時間詞
V	Verb	動詞
Pro	Pronoun	代名詞
Prep	Preposition	介詞
Conj	Conjunction	連接詞

Story

The fall semester will start soon. This year, Mark, Lin, Linda, Maria, Jennifer, and Jeff will become 10th grade students.

Mark and Lin are good friends. They are also teammates on the school basketball team. This year, their goal is to win the championship in high school basketball tournament. Linda and Maria are cheerleaders. They cheer for the basketball team very often.

Jennifer and Jeff are the president and vice president of the Kung Fu Club. Jennifer is practicing for the youth kung fu tournament. Jeff loves kung fu and many different aspects of Chinese culture.

There are two levels of Chinese classes this semester, basic level and intermediate level. Mark, Linda, and Maria are placed in the basic level class taught by teacher Daisy.

Characters

Mark

Mark was born in Boston. He loves sports, especially basketball. He is currently the captain of the high school basketball team. He likes his friends and is a very popular guy at school. His father works in an international trading company at New York and his mother is a housewife. His younger brother, Henry, is an 8th grade student at the same high school.

Lin moved to the States with his family when he was six years old. He has a sister, Wendy, and a brother, Lucas. He lives only a few blocks away from Mark, so they get together to play basketball every once in a while. Lin speaks Mandarin at home with his parents but his reading and writing abilities are not as good.

His parents are encouraging him to take more Mandarin courses. Lin will take an intermediate level Mandarin class this semester.

Linda is an African American student. Her father is a policeman and her mother is a nurse. Linda has two sisters, Ginny and Laura. Linda's hobby is painting. She wants to become a fashion designer in the future. Linda is a cheerleader of the basketball team. Her best friend is Maria.

Maria's parents moved to the States from Mexico when she was very young. She speaks both Spanish and English. Her hobbies are cooking and dancing. She loves Chinese food, especially the spicy Sichuan cuisine. She has a brother named Dominic and her sister is Olivia. Maria is also a cheerleader.

Jennifer

Jennifer's mom came from Shanghai. She speaks Mandarin with her mother at home. Jennifer's parents worked as computer engineers at Silicon Valley of California, and moved to New York just a couple of years ago. Jennifer started practicing martial arts when she was very young and has won several medals. Jennifer is not only passionate about martial arts, but also enjoys the great time she has with her masters and kung fu buddies. This semester, Jennifer will be a 10th grade student and she will also be the head of the kung fu club. Jennifer has a brother named Kevin.

Jeff's mother is a primary school teacher. He has been fascinated by Chinese kung fu ever since he was a kid. He is also interested in Chinese culture, especially Chinese chess and calligraphy. Chinese characters sometimes look like drawings or paintings to him. He took some Mandarin courses before and got good

Jeff

grades. This semester, he will take the intermediate level Mandarin course. His biggest dream is to travel to China in the future. Jeff is currently the vice-president of Kung Fu Club.

Contents

Contents

How Was Your Winter Vacation?
你的寒假過得怎麼樣？

Warm Up Activities

1. What did you do during the winter vacation? Where did you visit?
2. Did you have fun? Is there any experience that you would like to share with us?

LESSON 1

STORY

It is the first term of the year. Students are now back to school after the Christmas holidays. Today, the members of the Kung Fu club are gathering for the first practice session. The students are sharing with one another what they did during their vacation. Jennifer is showing the pictures of her trip to Shanghai on her laptop. Her cousin Zhang Han took her to the Bund, Yu Garden, where there is so much traditional Chinese architecture, and the City God Temple of Shanghai for some local food. Jennifer finds Shanghai an international city where there are more and more skyscrapers in the recent years. Wherever she went in Shanghai, there was always a vast crowd of people.

DIALOGUE

Jeff：你們好。好久不見，你們的寒假，過得怎麼樣？

你们好。好久不见，你们的寒假，过得怎么样？

Nǐmen hǎo。Hǎojiǔbújiàn，nǐmen de hánjià，guò de zěnmeyàng？

Jennifer：快過來，看我在上海拍的照片！

快过来，看我在上海拍的照片！

Kuài guò lái，kàn wǒ zài Shànghǎi pāi de zhàopiàn！

Mark：你去了好多地方，這是哪兒？好熱鬧。

你去了好多地方，这是哪儿？好热闹。

Nǐ qù le hǎoduō dìfāng，zhè shì nǎr？hǎo rènào。

Jennifer：這是上海最有名的豫園。

这是上海最有名的豫园。

Zhè shì Shànghǎi zuì yǒumíng de Yùyuán。

Lin：這些建築古色古香，真漂亮。

这些建筑古色古香，真漂亮。

Zhèxiē jiànzhú Gǔsègǔxiāng，zhēn piàoliàng。

Jennifer：附近的小吃更美味，尤其是小籠包，讓我念念不忘。

附近的小吃更美味，尤其是小笼包，让我念念不忘。

Fùjìn de xiǎochī gèng měiwèi，yóuqí shì Xiǎolóngbāo，ràng wǒ Niànniànbúwàng。

DISCUSSION

1. Where did Jennifer go during winter vacation?

2. What type of architecture can be seen in Yu Garden?

3. What is one of the things that Jennifer cannot forget?

VOCABULARY

	Traditional Character	Simplified Character	Pinyin	English
1	寒假 暑假	寒假 暑假	hánjià shǔjià	[名] winter vacation summer vacation
2	快	快	kuài	[副] hurry
3	過來	过来	guò lai	[動] come here
4	拍	拍	pāi	[動] take (photo)
5	地方	地方	dìfāng	[名] place
6	熱鬧	热闹	rènào	[形] crowded; busy
7	最	最	zuì	[副] most
8	這些	这些	zhè xiē	[代名] these
9	建築	建筑	jiànzhú	[名] building; architecture
10	古色古香	古色古香	Gǔsègǔxiāng	[形] traditional

	Traditional Character	Simplified Character	Pinyin	English
11	小吃	小吃	xiǎochī	[名] snack
12	更	更	gèng	[副] even more
13	美味	美味	měiwèi	[形] delicious; tasty
14	尤其是	尤其是	yóuqí shì	[副] especially
15	讓	让	ràng	[介] to cause

TERM

	Traditional Character	Simplified Character	Pinyin	English
1	豫園	豫园	Yùyuán	Yu Garden
2	小籠包	小笼包	Xiǎolóngbāo	Xiaolongbao

EXPRESSION

	Traditional Character	Simplified Character	Pinyin	English
1	好久不見	好久不见	hǎojiǔbújiàn	It's been so long
2	怎麼樣	怎么样	zěnmeyàng	How is it?
3	念念不忘	念念不忘	Niànniànbúwàng	unforgettable

GRAMMAR

1. N. , V.+得怎麼樣？

Examples:

你的中文課，學得怎麼樣？

你的中文课，学得怎么样？

Nǐ de Zhōngwénkè，xué de zěnmeyàng？

2. DirV+來/去

Examples:

桌子上有蛋糕，快過來吃吧。

桌子上有蛋糕，快过来吃吧。

Zhuōzi shàng yǒu dàngāo，kuài guòlai chī ba。

你什麼時候回去？

你什么时候回去？

Nǐ shénme shíhòu huíqù？

3. 更+adj

Examples:

這件旗袍，白色比黑色更漂亮。

这件旗袍，白色比黑色更漂亮。

Zhè jiàn qípáo，báisè bǐ hēisè gèng piàoliang。

她漂亮，她妹妹更漂亮。

她漂亮，她妹妹更漂亮。

Tā piàoliàng，tā mèimei gèng piàoliang。

LESSON 2

STORY

Lin went back to Taiwan during the winter vacation, and he took Mark with him. Lin shows his classmates some photos of Taiwan on his phone. Mark says they saw the Taipei 101 New Year fireworks and visited the famous National Palace Museum; in addition to that, there was one day that they hiked in the mountains in the morning, bathed in the hot spring in the afternoon, and then went to the night market for dinner. After dinner, they went up to the mountains again for the gorgeous night view and had hot tea together. All the photos of the food look inviting. Mark thinks that the life in Taipei is convenient and wonderful. They had so much fun!

DIALOGUE

Jeff： Mark，聽說寒假你跟Lin一起去了臺北？

　　　 Mark，听说寒假你跟Lin一起去了台北？

　　　 Mark，tīngshuō hánjià nǐ gēn lín yīqǐ qù le Táiběi？

Mark： 對，臺北真是一個有趣的城市。早上逛博物館，晚上逛夜市。

　　　 对，台北真是一个有趣的城市。早上逛博物馆，晚上逛夜市。

　　　 Duì，Táiběi zhēnshì yí ge yǒuqù de chéngshì。Zǎoshang guàng Bówùguǎn，wǎnshang guàng yèshì。

Jennifer：我看到你傳到網路上的照片，好像玩得很高興。

我看到你传到网络上的照片，好像玩得很高兴。

Wǒ kàndào nǐ chuán dào wǎnglù shàng de zhàopiàn，hǎoxiàng wán de hěn gāoxìng。

Lin：我表弟天天帶我們去不同的地方，不是上山喝茶，就是去泡溫泉。

我表弟天天带我们去不同的地方，不是上山喝茶，就是去泡温泉。

Wǒ biǎodì tiāntiān dài wǒmen qù bùtóng de dìfāng，bùshì shàng shān hē chá，jiùshì qù pào wēnquán。

Jeff：真有意思，希望暑假也能跟你們一塊兒去臺北和上海。

真有意思，希望暑假也能跟你们一块儿去台北和上海。

Zhēnyǒuyì si，xīwàng shǔjià yě néng gēn nǐmen yíkuàir qù Táiběi hàn shànghǎi。

DISCUSSION

1. What did Mark do during winter vacation?
2. How does Jennifer know that Mark had fun?
3. What places in Taipei did they visit?
4. What does Jeff hope?

VOCABULARY

	Traditional Character	Simplified Character	Pinyin	English
1	城市	城市	chéngshì	[名] city
2	早上	早上	zǎoshang	[名] morning
	晚上	晚上	wǎnshang	[名] evening; night
3	逛	逛	guàng	[動] stroll
4	網路	网络	wǎnglù	[名] internet
5	帶	带	dài	[動] take (a person somewhere)
6	不同	不同	bùtóng	[形] different
7	上山	上山	shàng shān	[動] go to the mountains
8	喝	喝	hē	[動] drink
9	茶	茶	chá	[名] tea
10	希望	希望	xīwàng	[動] hope

TERM

	Traditional Character	Simplified Character	Pinyin	English
1	博ㄅㄛ物ㄨˋ館ㄍㄨㄢˇ	博物馆	bówùguǎn	museum
2	夜ㄧㄝˋ市ㄕˋ	夜市	yèshì	night market
3	表ㄅㄧㄠˇ弟ㄉㄧˋ	表弟	biǎodì	cousin (male, younger, either from your mother's family or your father's sister's family)
4	泡ㄆㄠˋ溫ㄨㄣ泉ㄑㄩㄢˊ	泡温泉	pào wēnquán	hot spring bathing

EXPRESSION

	Traditional Character	Simplified Character	Pinyin	English
1	天ㄊㄧㄢ天ㄊㄧㄢ	天天	tiāntiān	everyday
2	一ㄧˊ塊ㄎㄨㄞˋ兒ㄦ	一块儿	yíkuàir	together

GRAMMAR

1. V+到

Examples:

你的照片，我傳到你的手機了。

你的照片，我传到你的手机了。

Nǐ de zhàopiàn，wǒ chuándào nǐ de shǒujī le。

我的東西，明天可以送到臺北嗎？

我的东西，明天可以送到台北吗？

Wǒ de dōngxi，míngtiān kěyǐ sòng dào Táiběi ma？

2. 好像+adj

Examples:

妹妹好像很高興。

妹妹好像很高兴。

Mèimei hǎoxiàng hěn gāoxìng。

3. 不是…就是…

Examples:

我暑假不是去上海，就是去臺北。

我暑假不是去上海，就是去台北。

Wǒ shǔjià búshì qù Shànghǎi，jiùshì qù Táiběi。

I. PRACTICE

1.

Q：你的中文，學得怎麼樣？

你的中文，学得怎么样？

Nǐ de Zhōngwén xué de zěnmeyàng？

A：非常有趣。

非常有趣。

Fēicháng yǒuqù。

Practice

Q：你週末過得怎麼樣？

你周末过得怎么样？

Nǐ zhōumò guò de zěnmeyàng？

→A：＿＿＿＿＿＿＿＿＿

2.

Q：我可以進去嗎？

我可以进去吗？

Wǒ kěyǐ jìn qù ma？

A：請進來。

请进来。

Qǐng jìn lái。

Practice

Q：你可以過來幫我嗎？

你可以过来帮我吗？

nǐ kěyǐ guò lái bāng wǒ ma？

→A：＿＿＿＿＿＿＿＿＿

3.

Q：這張照片，請你傳到我的手機，可以嗎？

这张照片，请你传到我的手机，可以吗？

Zhè zhāng zhàopiàn，qǐng nǐ chuándào wǒ de shǒujī，kěyǐ ma？

A：你的照片，我已經傳到你的手機了。

你的照片，我已经传到你的手机了。

Nǐ de zhàopiàn，wǒ yǐjīng chuándào nǐ de shǒujī le。

Practice

Q：吃的東西，可以帶到博物館裡嗎？

吃的东西，可以带到博物馆里吗？

chīde dōngxi，kěyǐ dài dào bówùguǎn lǐ ma？

→A：_____

4.

Q：你寒假要去哪裡？

你寒假要去哪里？

Nǐ hánjià yào qù nǎlǐ？

A：不是上海就是臺北。

不是上海就是台北。

Búshì Shànghǎi jiùshì Táiběi。

Practice

Q：週末，你要做什麼？

周末，你要做什么？

Zhōumò，nǐ yào zuòshénme？

→A：_____

II. EXERCISE

1. Complete the following dialogues

A：你這個週末過得怎麼樣？

你这个周末过得怎么样？

Nǐ zhège zhōumò guòde zěnmeyàng？

B：_____ 。

A：_____。

B：不是去吃飯，就是去逛夜市。

不是去吃饭，就是去逛夜市。

Bú shì qù chīfàn，jiùshì qù guàng yèshì。

2. Complete the following task

Prepare some photos you took when you traveled. Introduce to the class the culture and characteristics of the place.

III. SUPPLEMENTARY EXPLANATION

◎假

Vacation	寒假 寒假	暑假 暑假	春假 春假	年假 年假	病假 病假	事假 事假
Pinyin	hánjià	shǔjià	chūn jià	nián jià	bìngjià	shì jià
English	winter break	summer break	Chinese spring break	Chinese New Year break	sick leave	personal leave

◎節慶

Holiday	春節 春节	元宵節 元宵节	端午節 端午节	中秋節 中秋节	清明節 清明节	中元節 中元节	聖誕節 圣诞节	感恩節 感恩节
Pinyin	Chūn jié	Yuán xiāo jié	Duān wǔ jié	Zhōng qiū jié	Qīng míng jié	Zhōng yuán jié	Shèngdàn jié	Gǎnēnjié
English	Chinese New Year/ Spring Festival	Lantern Festival	Dragon Boat Festival	Mid-Autumn Festival	Tomb Sweeping Day	Hungry Ghost Festival	Christmas	Thanksgiving

◎臺灣小吃

Food	小籠包 小笼包	臭豆腐 臭豆腐	牛肉麵 牛肉面	炒米粉 炒米粉	燒餅油條 烧饼油条	豆漿 豆浆	鳳梨酥 凤梨酥	珍珠奶茶 珍珠奶茶
Pinyin	Xiǎo lóng bāo	Chòu dòufu	Niú ròu miàn	Chǎo mǐfěn	Shāo bǐng yóu tiáo	Dòu jiāng	Fèng lí sū	Zhēn zhū nǎi chá
English	xiaolong-bao/ steamed meat buns	Stinky Tofu	Beef Noodle Soup	Fried rice noodles	Fried dough stick wrapped in a baked roll	Soy-bean Milk	Pineapple cake	Bubble Tea/ Pearl milk tea/Boba

IV. CULTURAL NOTES

1. Yu Garden（豫園）

Situated in Shanghai's city center, Yu Garden is a very well known park that boasts shopping streets and temples for tutelary deities within the ground's premises. The site is always bustling and it is a must-see for travelers. Completed in 1559 during the Ming dynasty, Yu Garden is a historic park of that was once belonged to a single proprietor. Ownership has since changed hands many times over the last 100 years and is now open to the public. In the vicinity are many restaurants that serve up Shanghainese food and there are lots of shops that have retained a traditional feel, attracting tourists from far and wide.

2. National Palace Museum（故宮博物院）

There are over 700,000 cultural relics stored at the National Palace Museum in Taipei City, Taiwan. Spanning dates from 10th century BC all the way up to the Qing dynasty, among the relics are jade stones, ceramics, paintings, calligraphy, and many other works – the world's most prized collection of ancient Chinese art. The collection was initially amassed 800 years ago by a Song dynasty emperor and later stored in the Forbidden City in Beijing. The aggregate works were moved around during both the Second World War and the Chinese Civil War, but in 1949 found a final resting place in Taiwan without a single piece having been left behind. The National Palace Museum has seen over 4.5 million visitors, sometimes more than ten thousand per day, making it the 7th most trafficked art museum in the world.

Here's Something for You

這是一點小禮物！

Warm Up Activities

1. Would you bring your friends and family gifts if you were to travel aboard?

2. What kind of souvenirs would you get if you were to travel abroad?

LESSON 1

STORY

　　Jennifer bought some Chinese Zodiac animal key chains in Shanghai as gifts to her friends. She asked the store to carve her friends' names on them. Jeff's key chain is different because he is one year younger.

DIALOGUE

Jennifer：這是我從上海帶來的小禮物，一人一個。

這是我从上海带来的小礼物，一人一个。

Zhè shì wǒ cóng Shànghǎi dài lái de xiǎo lǐwù，yì rén yí ge。

Mark：好可愛的鑰匙圈，上面還有我的名字！謝謝！

好可爱的钥匙圈，上面还有我的名字！谢谢！

Hǎo kěài de yàoshi quān，shàng miàn hái yǒu wǒ de míng-zi！xièxie！

Jeff：咦，你們的動物都是老虎，爲什麼我的是兔子？

咦，你们的动物都是老虎，为什么我的是兔子？

Yí，nǐmen de dòngwù dōu shì lǎohǔ，wèishénme wǒ de shì tùzi？

Lin：因爲你比我們小一歲！

因为你比我们小一岁！

Yīnwèi nǐ bǐ wǒmen xiǎo yí suì！

Jennifer 這是中國的生肖，我們17歲屬虎，你16歲屬兔！

這是中国的生肖，我们17岁属虎，你16岁属兔！

Zhè shì Zhōngguó de shēngxiào，wǒmen shíqī suì shǔ hǔ，nǐ shíliù suì shǔ tù！

DISCUSSION

1. What did Jennifer bring from Shanghai?
2. What is special about the gifts?
3. Why is Jeff's gift different from the others' gifts?

VOCABULARY

	Traditional Character	Simplified Character	Pinyin	English
1	帶來	带来	dàilái	[動] bring
2	禮物	礼物	lǐwù	[名] gift
3	鑰匙 鑰匙圈	钥匙 钥匙圈	yàoshi yàoshi quān	[名] key key chain
4	上面	上面	shàngmiàn	[名] on
5	還有	还有	hái yǒu	[副] also
6	動物	动物	dòngwù	[名] animal
7	比	比	bǐ	[介] a preposition used to make comparison
8	小 大	小 大	xiǎo dà	[形] young; small; little old;big;large
9	屬	属	shǔ	[動] belong to

TERM

	Traditional Character	Simplified Character	Pinyin	English
1	老虎 虎	老虎 虎	lǎohǔ hǔ	tiger tiger
2	兔子 兔	兔子 兔	tùzi tù	rabbit rabbit
3	生肖	生肖	shēngxiào	Chinese Zodiac

EXPRESSION

	Traditional Character	Simplified Character	Pinyin	English
1	咦	咦	yí	similar to the expression of hmm; huh
2	因為	因为	yīnwèi	because

GRAMMAR

1. 從＋地方＋動詞＋來

Examples:

我從上海帶來了禮物。

我从上海带来了礼物。

Wǒ cóng Shànghǎi dài lái le lǐwù。

我從學校回來了。

我从学校回来了。

Wǒ cóng xuéxiào huílái le。

2. 數詞+量詞+數詞+量詞

　　Examples:

　　　　鳳梨酥，一人一個。

　　　　凤梨酥，一人一个。

　　　　Fènglí sū，yì rén yí ge。

　　　　蛋糕，一個一塊錢。

　　　　蛋糕，一个一块钱。

　　　　Dàngāo，yí ge yí kuài qián。

3. 名詞+比+名詞+形容詞+數詞+量詞

　　Examples:

　　　　我比你小一歲。

　　　　我比你小一岁。

　　　　Wǒ bǐ nǐ xiǎo yí suì。

　　　　寒假比暑假少一個月。

　　　　寒假比暑假少一个月。

　　　　Hánjià bǐ shǔjià shǎo yí ge yuè。

LESSON 2

STORY

Today is the first day of class for elementary level Chinese. Mark, Linda, and Maria are all enrolled for this term. Mark brings with him some local Taiwanese cuisine – some pineapple cakes and suncakes for Linda and Maria to have a taste. Linda thinks it is interesting that there are suncakes and also mooncakes in Taiwan.

DIALOGUE

Mark： 大家來嚐嚐，這是我從臺北帶來的特產。

大家来尝尝，这是我从台北带来的特产。

Dàjiā lái cháng cháng，zhè shì wǒ cóng Táiběi dài lái de tèchǎn。

Linda： 這是什麼？味道很特別！

这是什么？味道很特别！

Zhè shì shénme？wèidào hěn tèbié！

Mark： 方形的是「鳳梨酥」，是用鳳梨做的點心。圓的叫「太陽餅」，是臺灣中部的名產。

方形的是「凤梨酥」，是用凤梨做的点心。圆的叫「太阳饼」，是台湾中部的名产。

Fāng xíng de shì 「Fènglísū」，shì yòng fènglí zuò de diǎnxīn。Yuán de jiào 「Tàiyángbǐng」，shì Táiwān zhōng bù de míngchǎn。

Maria：我以前吃過月餅，很好吃。這個太陽餅，甜甜的，也很好吃。

我以前吃过月饼，很好吃。这个太阳饼，甜甜的，也很好吃。

Wǒ yǐqián chī guò yuèbǐng，hěn hǎo chī。Zhè ge tàiyángbǐng，tián tián de，yě hěn hǎo chī。

DISCUSSION

1. What does the cake Mark brought from Taipei taste like?
2. What is the difference between a pineapple cake and a suncake?

VOCABULARY

	Traditional Character	Simplified Character	Pinyin	English
1	嚐嚐	尝尝	cháng cháng	[動] taste
2	特產	特产	tèchǎn	[名] local cuisine; specialty
3	味道	味道	wèidào	[名] taste
4	特別	特别	tèbié	[形] special
5	方形	方形	fāng xíng	[名] square
6	圓形 圓	圆形 圆	yuán xíng yuán	[名] circle circle
7	用	用	yòng	[動] similar to the expression of "with"
8	點心	点心	diǎnxīn	[名] light refreshment
9	中部	中部	zhōng bù	[名] the middle part of an area
10	名產	名产	míngchǎn	[名] specialty goods

	Traditional Character	Simplified Character	Pinyin	English
11	以ˇ前ㄑㄧㄢˊ	以前	yǐqián	[名] a point of time before
12	甜ㄊㄧㄢˊ	甜	tián	[形] sweet

TERM

	Traditional Character	Simplified Character	Pinyin	English
1	鳳ㄈㄥˋ梨ㄌㄧˊ酥ㄙㄨ	凤梨酥	Fènglísū	pineapple cake
2	鳳ㄈㄥˋ梨ㄌㄧˊ	凤梨	fènglí	pineapple
3	月ㄩㄝˋ餅ㄅㄧㄥˇ	月饼	yuèbǐng	Moon cake
4	太ㄊㄞˋ陽ㄧㄤˊ餅ㄅㄧㄥˇ	太阳饼	Tàiyángbǐng	Suncake

GRAMMAR

1. 來+V

Examples:

請來嚐嚐我做的蛋糕。

请来尝尝我做的蛋糕。

Qǐnglái cháng cháng wǒ zuò de dàngāo。

來看看我拍的照片吧！

来看看我拍的照片吧！

Lái kànkàn wǒ pāi de zhàopiàn ba！

2. 是用+N+V+的

Examples:

這是用鳳梨做的。

这是用凤梨做的。

Zhè shì yòng fènglí zuò de。

這個餅乾是用茶做的。

这个饼干是用茶做的。

Zhège bǐnggān shì yòng chá zuò de。

3. 形容詞重疊+的

Examples:

太陽餅甜甜的。

太阳饼甜甜的。

Tàiyángbǐng tián tián de。

這個博物館小小的，可是很有趣。

这个博物馆小小的，可是很有趣。

Zhège bówùguǎn xiǎoxiǎo de，kěshì hěn yǒuqù。

I. PRACTICE

1.

Q：你是從哪裡過來的？

你是从哪里过来的？

Nǐ shì cóng nǎlǐ guòlái de？

A：我是從學校過來的。

我是从学校过来的。

Wǒ shì cóng xuéxiào guòlái de。

Practice

Q： 這照片是從哪裡傳來的？
这照片是从哪里传来的？
zhè zhàopiàn shì cóng nǎlǐ chuán lái de？

→A：＿＿＿＿＿＿＿＿＿＿＿＿

2.

Q：這件衣服的尺寸合適嗎？
这件衣服的尺寸合适吗？
Zhè jiàn yīfú de chǐcùn héshì ma？

A：有沒有比這件小一號的衣服？
有没有比这件小一号的衣服？
Yǒuméiyǒu bǐ zhè jiàn xiǎo yí hào de yīfú？

Practice

Q： 你姊姊比你大幾歲？
你姊姊比你大几岁？
Nǐ jiějie bǐ nǐ dà jǐ suì？

→A：＿＿＿＿＿＿＿＿＿＿＿＿

3.

Q：這個月餅好吃嗎？
这个月饼好吃吗？
Zhè ge yuèbǐng hǎochī ma？

A：甜甜的，我很喜歡。
甜甜的，我很喜欢。
Tián tián de，wǒ hěn xǐhuān。

Practice

Q： 這道菜的味道怎麼樣？

這道菜的味道怎么样？

Zhè dào cài de wèidào zěnmeyàng？

→A： _____

II. EXERCISE

1. Complete the following dialogues

A：你們兩個誰比較大？

你们两个谁比较大？

Nǐmen liǎng ge shéi bǐjiào dà？

B： _____ 。

A：鳳梨的味道怎麼樣？

凤梨的味道怎么样？

Fènglí de wèidào zěnmeyàng？

B： _____ 。

2. Complete the following task

1. Introduce a local cuisine from your hometown.

2. On the Internet, find out the Chinese Zodiac signs that your family members belong to.

III. SUPPLEMENTARY EXPLANATION

1. 生肖

Zodiac	鼠 鼠	牛 牛	虎 虎	兔 兔	龍 龙	蛇 蛇
Pinyin	shǔ	niú	hǔ	tù	lóng	shé
English	rat	ox	tiger	rabbit	dragon	snake
Zodiac	馬 马	羊 羊	猴 猴	雞 鸡	狗 狗	豬 猪
Pinyin	mǎ	yáng	hóu	jī	gǒu	zhū
English	horse	goat	monkey	rooster	dog	pig

2. 補充問句：

A：What is your Chinese zodiac sign?

你是屬什麼的？

你是属什么的？

B：My Chinese zodiac sign is ＿＿＿＿＿＿＿＿.

我是屬「 」的。

我是属「 」的。

IV. CULTURAL NOTES

1. Chinese Gift-giving Etiquette（送禮的文化）

Everyone likes gifts and the Chinese are no exception. Do you know what kinds of gifts you should bring when visiting Chinese friends? Food is always a good idea. Fruits, cookies, cake, and wine are all wonderful options. If you are to bring fruit, it is better to bring "exquisite", exported fruits.

A few certain items are not ideal options: clock, umbrella, fan, are all taboos. It has to do with the pronunciation of the names of these items. 送鐘 (sòngzhōng, give clock) sounds exactly the same as 送終 (sòngzhōng), which means accompanying someone who is dying or attending a funeral. 傘 (sǎn, umbrella) and 扇 (shàn, fan) both sound like 散, which means separation.

Be aware not to open the gift in front of the giver no matter how excited you are having received the gift. Opening a gift upon receiving is considered impolite in the Chinese culture.

2. Twelve Chinese Zodiac Signs（十二生肖）

The Chinese zodiac is not exclusive to the Chinese culture. It is shared by some other ethnic groups, such as the Vietnamese. The order of Chinese zodiac signs is: rat, ox, tiger, rabbit, dragon, snake, horse, goat, monkey, rooster, dog, and pig. Originally, it is used as a way to document years. One year is ruled by one animal, and 12 years is a loop. Asking people which sign they belong to is a polite way to learn about their age.

There are superstitions related to the Chinese zodiac signs, and this is part of the Chinese fortune-telling culture. The Chinese believe that each sign has its own characteristics that would affect the person born of the year it is ruling. It is also believed that the zodiac year of one's birth would bring the person bad luck throughout the entire year; many would thus worship in the local temples in the hope of changing the fortune for the better.

第三章
UNIT 3

Happy New Year!

新年快樂！

Warm Up Activities

1. How do you welcome a new year? Have you ever celebrated Chinese New Year? If yes, what impressed you the most?
2. Do you know the lucky color of the Chinese New Year, and do you know why?

LESSON 1

STORY

The Chinese New Year is fast approaching. Much like Thanksgiving and Christmas, Chinese New Year is the time of the year when all the family members gather together. Ms. Lee used to study in China. In today's class, she shares her own experience of the Chinese New Year with the students. She also introduces some of the typical Chinese New Year greetings.

DIALOGUE

Ms. Lee：同學們好，下星期一是中國新年！

同学们好，下星期一是中国新年！

Tóngxué men hǎo，xià xīngqí yī shì Zhōngguó xīnnián！

Mark：在中國，怎麼慶祝新年？

在中国，怎么庆祝新年？

Zài Zhōngguó，zěnme qìngzhù xīnnián？

Ms. Lee：跟聖誕節一樣，在新年的前一天晚上，全家人要在一起吃晚飯。

跟圣诞节一样，在新年的前一天晚上，全家人要在一起吃晚饭。

Gēn shèngdànjié yíyàng，zài xīnnián de qián yì tiān wǎnshang，quánjiārén yào zài yìqǐ chī wǎn fàn。

Linda：有特別的活動嗎？

有特别的活动吗？

Yǒu tèbié de huódòng ma？

Ms. Lee：大家吃完晚飯，就一起聊天，整個晚上都不睡覺！到第二天早上，看到人就說：「恭喜！恭喜！」

大家吃完晚饭，就一起聊天，整个晚上都不睡觉！到第二天早上，看到人就说：「恭喜！恭喜！」

Dàjiā chī wán wǎnfàn，jiù yìqǐ liáotiān，zhěng ge wǎnshang dōu bú shuìjiào！Dào dì èr tiān zǎoshang，kàn dào rén jiù shuō：「Gōngxǐ！Gōngxǐ！」

DISCUSSION

1. How is Chinese New Year celebrated in China?

2. What are some of the events or activities during the New Year?

VOCABULARY

	Traditional Character	Simplified Character	Pinyin	English
1	同學	同学	tóngxué	[名] student; classmate
2	慶祝	庆祝	qìngzhù	[動] celebrate
3	有趣	有趣	yǒuqù	[形] interesting
4	全家	全家	quán jiā	[名] the whole family
5	晚飯	晚饭	wǎn fàn	[名] dinner
6	活動	活动	huódòng	[名] event; activity
7	完	完	wán	[動] finish, end
8	聊天	聊天	liáotiān	[動] chat
9	整個	整个	zhěng ge	[形] whole; entire
10	睡覺	睡觉	shuìjiào	[動] sleep

TERM

	Traditional Character	Simplified Character	Pinyin	English
1	中國新年	中国新年	Zhōngguó xīn nián	Chinese New Year; Lunar New Year
2	聖誕節	圣诞节	Shèngdànjié	Christmas
3	恭喜	恭喜	gōngxǐ	an expression used to wish others a good luck; similar to congratulations

EXPRESSION

	Traditional Character	Simplified Character	Pinyin	English
1	跟… 一樣	跟…一样	gēn…yíyàng	like; as
2	前一天	前一天	qián yì tiān	the day before
3	第二天	第二天	dì èr tiān	second day

GRAMMAR

1. 跟…一樣

Examples:

我的名字跟他一樣。

我的名字跟他一样。

Wǒ de míngzi gēn tā yíyàng。

我跟她一樣是學生。

我跟她一样是学生。

Wǒ gēn tā yíyàng shì xuéshēng。

2. Verb+完+Noun，就+Verb

Examples:

我們吃完晚飯，就一起聊天。

我们吃完晚饭，就一起聊天。

Wǒmen chī wán wǎn fàn，jiù yìqǐ liáotiān。

我上完課，就回家。

我上完课，就回家。

Wǒ shàng wán kè，jiù huí jiā。

LESSON 2

STORY

During club time, assistant captain Jeff invited the intermediate level teacher Ms. Chen to teach the students calligraphic writing on spring festival couplets. Ms. Chen is from Taiwan. She writes beautiful calligraphy and also does ink-wash painting. Ms. Chen explains the meaning of each character as she writes. The students are all excited. They cut the paper and grind the inkstick against the inkstone carefully so the ink does not splash. On the table are brushes, ink, paper, inkstones, as well as pieces of red paper. The atmosphere of the Chinese New Year fills the classroom.

DIALOGUE

Jeff：今天謝謝陳老師特別抽空來教我們寫春聯！

今天谢谢陈老师特别抽空来教我们写春联！

Jīntiān xièxie Chén lǎoshī tèbié chōukòng lái jiāo wǒmen xiě chūnlián！

Ms. Chen：新年快要到了，今天教大家寫幾個字，可以貼在門上！

新年快要到了，今天教大家写几个字，可以贴在门上！

Xīnnián kuàiyào dào le，jīntiān jiāo dàjiā xiě jǐ ge zì，kě yǐ tiē zài mén shàng！

Lin：我以前寫過書法，可是寫得不好看。

我以前写过书法，可是写得不好看。

Wǒ yǐqián xiě guò shūfǎ，kěshì xiě de bù hǎo kàn。

Ms. Chen：我準備了紅紙和毛筆，現在一人拿一張紅紙和一枝毛筆。我們寫一個「春」字。

我准备了红纸和毛笔，现在一人拿一张红纸和一枝毛笔。我们写一个「春」字。

Wǒ zhǔnbèi le hóngzhǐ hàn máobǐ，xiànzài yì rén ná yì zhāng hóng zhǐ hàn yì zhī máo bǐ。Wǒmen xiě yí ge 「chūn」zì。

Jenny：我知道，這是「春天來了」的意思。

我知道，这是「春天来了」的意思。

Wǒ zhīdào，zhè shì 「chūntiān lái le」de yìsi。

DISCUSSION

1. What did Ms. Chen teach the students?

2. What did Ms. Chen prepare?

3. What characters did the students write and why?

VOCABULARY

	Traditional Character	Simplified Character	Pinyin	English
1	抽ㄔㄡ空ㄎㄨㄥ	抽空	chōukòng	[動] to allocate time for something
2	寫ㄒㄧㄝ	写	xiě	[動] write
3	字ㄗ	字	zì	[名] word; character
4	貼ㄊㄧㄝ	贴	tiē	[動] stick
5	門ㄇㄣ	门	mén	[名] door
6	準ㄓㄨㄣ備ㄅㄟ	准备	zhǔnbèi	[動] prepare
7	紅ㄏㄨㄥ	红	hóng	[形] red
8	紙ㄓ	纸	zhǐ	[名] paper
9	現ㄒㄧㄢ在ㄗㄞ	现在	xiànzài	[副] now
10	拿ㄋㄚ	拿	ná	[動] take

	Traditional Character	Simplified Character	Pinyin	English
11	枝ㄓ	枝	zhī	[量] a measure word used to count pens
12	春ㄔㄨㄣ 天ㄊㄧㄢ	春天	chūntiān	[名] spring
13	意ㄧ 思ㄙ	意思	yìsi	[名] meaning

TERM

	Traditional Character	Simplified Character	Pinyin	English
1	春ㄔㄨㄣ 聯ㄌㄧㄢˊ	春联	chūnlián	spring festival cou-plet
2	書ㄕㄨ 法ㄈㄚˇ	书法	shūfǎ	calligraphy
3	毛ㄇㄠˊ 筆ㄅㄧˇ	毛笔	máobǐ	brush

EXPRESSION

	Traditional Character	Simplified Character	Pinyin	English
1	可ㄎㄜˇ 是ㄕˋ	可是	kěshì	but

GRAMMAR

1. **Verb+在+地方**

Examples:

這張春聯，請貼在門上。

这张春联，请贴在门上。

Zhè zhāng chūnlián，qǐng tiē zài mén shàng。

你的名字，請寫在這裡。

你的名字，请写在这里。

Nǐ de míngzi，qǐng xiě zài zhèlǐ。

2. ···,可是···

Examples:

我學過中文，可是說得不好。

我学过中文，可是说得不好。

Wǒ xué guò Zhōngwén，kěshì shuō de bù hǎo。

我喜歡做飯，可是做得不好吃。

我喜欢做饭，可是做得不好吃。

Wǒ xǐhuān zuò fàn，kěshì zuò de bù hǎo chī。

I. PRACTICE

1.

Q：這道菜的味道怎麼樣？

这道菜的味道怎么样？

Zhè dào cài de wèidào zěnmeyàng？

A：跟我媽媽做的差不多。

跟我妈妈做的差不多。

Gēn wǒ māma zuò de chàbuduō。

Practice

Q：上海的冬天很冷嗎？

上海的冬天很冷吗？

Shànghǎi de dōngtiān hěn lěng ma？

→A：_____

2.

Q：你什麼時候回家？

你什么时候回家？

Nǐ shénme shíhòu huíjiā？

A：我練習完，就回家。

我练习完，就回家。

Wǒ liànxí wán，jiù huíjiā。

Practice

Q：你們什麼時候去看電影？

你们什么时候去看电影？

Nǐmen shénme shíhòu qù kàn diànyǐng？

→A：_____

3.

Q：他的名字，你寫在哪裡？

他的名字，你写在哪里？

Tā de míngzi，nǐ xiě zài nǎlǐ？

A：我寫在紙上。

我写在纸上。

Wǒ xiě zài zhǐ shàng。

Practice

Q：這張照片，應該貼在哪裡？

这张照片，应该贴在哪里？

Zhè zhāng zhàopiàn，yīnggāi tiē zài nǎlǐ？

→A：＿＿＿＿＿＿＿＿＿

II. EXERCISE

1. Complete the following dialogues

A：這裡的東西比較貴吧！

这里的东西比较贵吧！

Zhèlǐ de dōngxi bǐ jiào guì ba！

B：跟紐約的＿＿＿＿＿＿。

跟纽约的＿＿＿＿＿＿。

Gēn Niǔyuē de＿＿＿＿＿＿。

A：李老師的課比較難嗎？

李老师的课比较难吗？

Lǐlǎoshide kè bǐjiào nán ma？

B：＿＿＿＿＿＿＿＿＿。

A：他什麼時候回來？

他什么时候回来？

Tā shénme shíhòu huílai。

B：他＿＿＿完＿＿＿就回來。

他＿＿＿完＿＿＿就回来。

Tā＿＿＿wán＿＿＿jiù huílai。

A：你平常什麼時候睡覺？

你平常什么时候睡觉？

Nǐ píngcháng shénme shíhòu shuìjiào？

B：＿＿＿＿＿＿＿＿＿＿＿。

2. Complete the following task

Find some essential Chinese New Year dishes online, compare them with those of Christmas, and explain the reason why they are prepared during New Year.

III. SUPPLEMENTARY EXPLANATION

1. 文房四寶

Four Treasures of the Study	筆 笔	墨 墨	紙 纸	硯 砚
Pinyin	bǐ	mò	zhǐ	yàn
English	ink brush	Chinese ink; ink stick	paper	inkstone

2. 春聯

Auspicious words	春 春	福 福	恭喜發財 恭喜发财	大吉大利 大吉大利	萬事如意 万事如意
Pinyin	chūn	fú	Gōngxǐfācái	Dàjídàlì	Wànshìrúyì
English	spring	good fortune; luck; happiness	may you be prosperous; may you have a prosperous New Year	great auspice; good luck to you	wish you all the best

IV. CULTURAL NOTES

1. The Story of Nain（年獸的故事）

The Chinese New Year has a long history and there are many legends behind the various customs of the Chinese New Year. One of the most favored Chinese New Year legends is the story of "Nian". Once upon a time, there was a horrifying beast named "Nain". It would come out on New Year's Eve to look for animals, even human beings, to consume. Later, some discovered its weakness： color red, fire, and loud sounds were the three things that he was scared of. That is the reason why that, today, on New Year's Eve, every household would put up red paper couplets on the door and set off firecrackers. On New Year's Day, people would greet one another with "Congratulations!" for not having been eaten.

2. Chinese New Year Food and Customs（年菜跟習俗）

Chinese people from all over the world celebrate the Chinese New Year in slightly different ways, yet all hope for a reunion, good luck, and wealth. Some dishes are common for the Chinese New Year because of their pronunciations or appearances resemble auspices. For example： niangao means getting higher year by year, fish (yú) sounds like "surplus", and dumplings resemble a kind of ancient currency.

The day before the Chinese New Year, every household would do a thorough house-cleaning. Sweeping should not be done on New Year's Day for fear that good fortune and wealth will be swept away. During the Chinese New Year holidays, adults would give children some money in the red envelopes.

第四章
UNIT 4

What Are You Doing on New Year's Eve?
除夕時你要做什麼?

Warm Up Activities

1. Have you participated in any New Year's Eve party? If yes, was it fun?
2. If you are to hold a New Year's Eve party, what activities would you include?

LESSON 1

STORY

The Chinese New Year is not celebrated at school; however, every year a party is held on Chinese New Year's Eve. This year, Jeff the assistant captain of the Kung Fu club is hosting the party. Jeff is discussing with the elementary level teacher Ms. Lee concerning the performance. They decide to have the students from the elementary class sing a Chinese song as the ending performance.

DIALOGUE

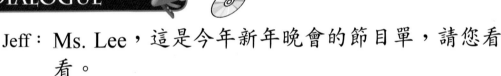

Jeff： Ms. Lee，這是今年新年晚會的節目單，請您看看。

Ms. Lee，這是今年新年晚会的节目单，请您看看。

Ms. Lee，zhè shì jīnnián xīnnián wǎnhuì de jiémù dān，qǐng nín kànkàn。

Ms. Lee：好，有中國武術，還有短劇。我覺得不錯。

好，有中国武术，还有短剧。我觉得不错。

Hǎo，yǒu Zhōngguó wǔshù，hái yǒu duǎn jù。Wǒ juéde búcuò。

Jeff：最後一個節目，您覺得唱歌好？還是表演好？

　　　最后一个节目，您觉得唱歌好？还是表演好？

　　　Zuìhòu yí ge jiémù，nín juéde chànggē hǎo？Hái shì biǎoyǎn hǎo？

Ms. Lee：初級班唱一首中文歌好了，大家也一起唱。

　　　　初级班唱一首中文歌好了，大家也一起唱。

　　　　Chūjí bān chàng yì shǒu zhōngwén gē hǎo le，dàjiā yě yìqǐ chàng。

Jeff：喔！還好我是主持人，不必唱歌！

　　　喔！还好我是主持人，不必唱歌！

　　　O！Háihǎo wǒ shì zhǔchírén，bùbì chàng gē！

DISCUSSION

1. What events/performances are in the party?
2. What did Jeff ask Ms. Lee?
3. What did Ms. Lee say about it?
4. Does Jeff like to sing?

VOCABULARY

	Traditional Character	Simplified Character	Pinyin	English
1	晚會	晚会	wǎnhuì	[名] party; event (usually held in the evening)
2	節目單	节目单	jiémù dān	[名] list of events
3	節目	节目	jiémù	[名] events
4	短劇	短剧	duǎn jù	[名] skit
5	最後	最后	zuìhòu	[副] at last
6	唱歌	唱歌	chàng gē	[動] sing
7	表演	表演	biǎoyǎn	[動] performance
8	初級班 班	初级班 班	chūjí bān bān	[名] elementary level; elementary class class
9	首	首	shǒu	[量] a measure word used to count songs

	Traditional Character	Simplified Character	Pinyin	English
10	還好	还好	háihǎo	[副] luckily
11	主持人	主持人	zhǔchí rén	[名] host; master of cer- emony
12	不必	不必	búbì	[副] not having to
13	喔	喔	ō	[語助] phew

TERM

	Traditional Character	Simplified Character	Pinyin	English
1	武術	武术	wǔshù	martial arts

GRAMMAR

1.  最後一+量+（**N**）

Examples:

最後一個節目是唱歌。

最后一个节目是唱歌。

Zuìhòu yí ge jiémù shì chànggē。

今天是我在臺北的最後一天。

今天是我在台北的最后一天。

Jīntiān shì wǒ zài Táiběi de zuìhòu yìtiān。

2. …好了

Examples:

晚上來我家聊天好了。

晚上来我家聊天好了。

Wǎnshang lái wǒ jiā liáotiān hǎo le。

我們去夜市吃小吃好了。

我们去夜市吃小吃好了。

Wǒmen qù yèshì chī xiǎochī hǎo le。

3. 還好…，…

Examples:

還好我是主持人，不必唱歌。

还好我是主持人，不必唱歌。

Háihǎo wǒ shì zhǔchí rén，búbì chànggē。

還好我會中文，去中國旅行沒問題。

还好我会中文，去中国旅行没问题。

Háihǎo wǒ huì Zhōngwén，qù Zhōngguó lǚxíng méi wèntí。

LESSON 2

STORY

The New Year's Eve party is so much fun! The music performance with traditional Chinese instruments creates an Oriental ambience. The skit presented by the intermediate level students wins a great round of applause. The Kung Fu club is up next performing martial arts. Jennifer, Mark, and Lin are all in the performance. The elementary level students are preparing for their Chinese song. Linda and Maria are watching Kung Fu club's performance from backstage while talking to each other.

DIALOGUE

Maria： Jennifer打拳打得眞好！

Jennifer打拳打得真好！

Jennifer dǎquán dǎ de zhēn hǎo！

Linda： 是啊，她每天最少練習兩個小時。

是啊，她每天最少练习两个小时。

Shì a，tā měitiān zuìshǎo liànxí liǎng ge xiǎoshí。

Maria： 難怪她打得這麼好！

难怪她打得这么好！

Nánguài tā dǎ de zhème hǎo！

Linda：現在輪到Lin跟Mark表演了！
現在轮到Lin跟Mark表演了！
Xiànzài lúndào Lin gēn Mark biǎoyǎn le！

Maria：你看！Mark踢得好高！唉呀！糟糕！他踢到Lin的鼻子了！
你看！Mark踢得好高！唉呀！糟糕！他踢到Lin的鼻子了！
Nǐ kàn！Mark tī de hǎo gāo！Ai ya！Zāogāo！Tā tī dào Lin de bízi le！

DISCUSSION

1. Why did Jennifer perform so well?
2. How was Mark and Lin's performance?

VOCABULARY

	Traditional Character	Simplified Character	Pinyin	English
1	打拳	打拳	dǎquán	[動] fight; do a specific kind of martial art
2	最少	最少	zuìshǎo	[副] at least
3	練習	练习	liànxí	[動] practice
4	小時	小时	xiǎoshí	[名] hour
5	難怪	难怪	nánguài	[副] no wonder
6	輪到	轮到	lúndào	[動] being someone's turn
7	跟	跟	gēn	[動] with
8	踢	踢	tī	[動] kick
9	高	高	gāo	[形] high
10	鼻子	鼻子	bízi	[名] nose

EXPRESSION

	Traditional Character	Simplifid Character	Pinyin	English
1	唉ㄞˊ呀ㄧ	唉呀	āiya	Oops
2	糟ㄗㄠ糕ㄍㄠ	糟糕	zāogāo	Oh No

GRAMMAR

1. 人+VOV得…

Examples:

Jennifer打拳打得眞好。

Jennifer打拳打得真好。

Jennifer dǎquán dǎ de zhēn hǎo。

Maria做菜做得眞好。

Maria做菜做得真好。

Maria zuòcài zuò de zhēn hǎo。

2. 輪到+人+V了

Examples:

現在輪到Mark表演了。

現在轮到Mark表演了。

Xiànzài lúndào Markbiǎoyǎn le。

現在輪到你說話了。

現在轮到你说话了。

Xiànzài lúndào nǐ shuōhuà le。

I. PRACTICE

1.

　Q：你覺得唱歌好？還是表演好？

　　你觉得唱歌好？还是表演好？

　　Nǐ juéde chànggē hǎo？Háishì biǎoyǎn hǎo？

　A：唱歌好了。

　　唱歌好了。

　　Chànggē hǎo le。

> **Practice**
>
> 　　Q：今天吃中國菜好？還是吃日本菜好？
>
> 　　今天吃中国菜好？还是吃日本菜好？
>
> 　　Jīntiān chī Zhōngguó cài hǎo？Háishì chī Rìběn cài hǎo？
>
> 　→A：＿＿＿＿＿＿＿＿＿＿

2.

　Q：Jennifer打拳打得怎麼樣？

　　Jennifer打拳打得怎么样？

　　Jennifer dǎquán dǎ de zěnmeyàng？

　A：Jennifer打拳打得很好。

　　Jennifer打拳打得很好。

　　Jennifer dǎquán dǎ de hěn hǎo。

> **Practice**
>
> 　　Q：Maria做菜做得怎麼樣？
>
> 　　Maria做菜做得怎么样？
>
> 　　Maria zuòcài zuò de zěnmeyàng？
>
> 　→A：＿＿＿＿＿＿＿＿＿＿

3.

Q：他每天練習多久？
他每天练习多久？
Tā měitiān liànxí duōjiǔ？

A：他每天最少練習兩個小時。
他每天最少练习两个小时。
Tā měitiān zuìshǎo liànxí liǎng ge xiǎoshí。

Practice

Q：你每天學幾個中文字？
你每天学几个中文字？
Nǐ měitiān xué jǐ ge Zhōngwén zì？

→A：_____

4.

Q：現在輪到誰表演了？
现在轮到谁表演了？
Xiànzài lúndào shéi biǎoyǎn le？

A：輪到我們了。
轮到我们了。
Lúndào wǒmen le。

Practice

Q：今天輪到誰做飯？
今天轮到谁做饭？
Jīntiān lúndào shéi zuòfàn？

→A：_____

II. EXERCISE

1. Complete the following dialogues

A：你覺得吃中國菜好？還是吃日本菜好？

你觉得吃中国菜好？还是吃日本菜好？

Nǐ juéde chī Zhōngguó cài hǎo？Háishì chī Rìběn cài hǎo？

B：＿＿＿＿＿＿＿＿＿。

A：你寫字寫得怎麼樣？

你写字写得怎么样？

Nǐ xiězì xiě de zěnmeyàng？

B：＿＿＿＿＿＿＿＿＿。

A：你每天練習中文多久？

你每天练习中文多久？

Nǐ měitiān liànxí Zhōngwén duōjiǔ？

B：最少＿＿＿＿＿。

最少＿＿＿＿＿。

Zuìshǎo＿＿＿＿＿。

A：＿＿＿＿＿＿＿＿＿。

B：輪到Jeff了。

轮到Jeff了。

Lúndào Jeff le。

2. Complete the following task

A. Form a team of 3 to 4 students and plan for a New Year's Eve party. Make a poster with information such as the date, venue, and events then share with the class.

B. Have the students talk about one of the New Year's Eve parties they participated. What were some of their unforgettable experiences?

III. SUPPLEMENTARY EXPLANATION

（節選歌曲）

恭喜恭喜

作詞／作曲：陳歌辛

每條大街小巷　每個人的嘴裡
見面第一句話　就是恭喜恭喜
恭喜恭喜 恭喜你呀　恭喜恭喜 恭喜你

冬天一到盡頭　真是好的消息
溫暖的春風　就要吹醒大地
恭喜恭喜 恭喜你呀　恭喜恭喜 恭喜你
恭喜恭喜 恭喜你呀　恭喜恭喜 恭喜你

měi tiáo dàjiē xiǎoxiàng měi gè rén de zuǐ lǐ

jiàn miàn dìyīgōuhuà jiùshì gōngxǐ gōngxǐ

gōngxǐ gōngxǐ gōngxǐ nǐ yā gōngxǐ gōngxǐ gōngxǐ nǐ

dōngtiān yī dào jìntóu zhēnshì hǎo de xiāoxi

wēnnuǎn de chūnfēng jiù yào chuī xǐng dàdì

gōngxǐ gōngxǐ gōngxǐ nǐ yā gōngxǐ gōngxǐ gōngxǐ nǐ

gōngxǐ gōngxǐ gōngxǐ nǐ yā gōngxǐ gōngxǐ gōngxǐ nǐ

IV. CULTURAL NOTES

1. Weiya – Year-end Dinner Party（尾牙）

　　In the Taiwanese tradition, "zuoya" is to worship the earth god Tu Di Gong on the first and fifteenth days of the lunar month (some do it on the second and the sixteenth days). The very last zuoya of the year is on the sixteenth day of the twelfth month of the lunar calendar, and it is called "weiya". Around the day of "weiya", many companies would prepare wonderful banquets to thank their employees for a year's hard work. Attending such banquet is known as "chi (eat) weiya". Larger corporations usually also arrange lucky draw and various performances for the weiya dinner.

Weiya is also the opportunity for employers to fire some of the employees. There will be a chicken dish on the table and whoever is seated towards the chicken head will not continue working for the company in the coming year. However, to avoid unnecessary awkwardness, this custom is not as common now as before.

2.New Year's Gala（新年晚會）

The event that excites the Chinese the most on New Year's Eve is undoubtedly the Spring Festival Gala produced by China Central Television. It is a variety show that includes singing, drama, crosstalk, and folk performances. The viewership is always around a few hundred million. Thus, many celebrities deem the opportunity to be on the Gala as a great honor.

第五章
UNIT 5

Do You Like Kung Fu Movies?
你喜歡功夫片嗎？

Warm Up Activities

1. Which Kung Fu movies have you seen and which one is your favorite?
2. What are some of the differences between Asian and Western movies?

LESSON 1

A new action movie is about to come out. Many of the fighting scenes were shot in Shanghai. Jeff has three tickets for the premier and he wants to invite Lin to go with him. Lin asks Jennifer to join them. Jennifer knows Kung Fu and one side of her family is from Shanghai. She is going to enjoy this movie.

DIALOGUE

Jeff：Lin！最近有一部功夫片，聽說不錯，要不要一起去看？

Lin！最近有一部功夫片，听说不错，要不要一起去看？

Lin！Zuìjìn yǒu yí bù gōngfū piàn，tīngshuō búcuò，yàobúyào yìqǐ qù kàn？

Lin：好啊！什麼時候？我們約在哪裡碰面？

好啊！什么时候？我们约在哪里碰面？

Hǎo a！Shénme shíhòu？Wǒmen yuē zài nǎlǐ pèngmiàn？

Jeff：我跟你約這個星期五晚上六點，在電影院售票
口前面，怎麼樣？

我跟你约这个星期五晚上六点，在电影院售票
口前面，怎么样？

Wǒ gēn nǐ yuē zhè ge xīngqí wǔ wǎnshang liù diǎn，zài
diànyǐngyuàn shòupiàokǒu qián miàn，zěnme yàng？

Lin：好！對了！要不要約Jennifer一起去？

好！对了！要不要约Jennifer一起去？

Hǎo！Duìle！Yàobúyào yuē Jennifer yìqǐ qù？

Jeff：Jennifer？對呀！我怎麼沒想到？她喜歡中國功
夫，她一定對這部電影有興趣！

Jennifer？对呀！我怎么没想到？她喜欢中国功
夫，她一定对这部电影有兴趣！

Jennifer？Duìya！Wǒ zěnme méi xiǎngdào？Tā xǐ huān
Zhōngguó gōngfū，tā yídìng duì zhè bù diànyǐng yǒu
xìngqù！

DISCUSSION

1. What movie did Jeff invite Lin to?
2. When and where are they meeting up?
3. Why did Jeff think Jennifer would find it interesting too?

VOCABULARY

	Tradional Character	Simplufied Character	Pinyin	English
1	最近	最近	zuìjìn	[副] recently
2	部	部	bù	[量] measure word used to count movies
3	功夫片	功夫片	gōngfū piàn	[名] action movie
4	約	约	yuē	[動] invite
5	碰面	碰面	pèngmiàn	[動] meet
6	電影院	电影院	diànyǐngyuàn	[名] movie theater
7	售票口 門口 電影票	售票口 門口 電影票	shòupiàokǒu ménkǒu diànyǐng piào	[名] ticketing booth gate; door movie ticket
8	一定	一定	yídìng	[形] certainly
9	有興趣	有兴趣	yǒu xìngqù	[形] interested

EXPRESSION

	Traditional Character	Simplified Character	Pinyin	English
1	我ㄨㄛˇ怎ㄗㄣˇ麼ㄇㄜ˙沒ㄇㄟˊ想ㄒㄧㄤˇ到ㄉㄠˋ？	我怎么没想到？	wǒ zěnme méi xiǎngdào?	How could I not think of that?

GRAMMAR

1. A跟B約+時間/在地方

Examples:

我跟你約早上十點。

我跟你约早上十点。

Wǒ gēn nǐ yuē zǎoshang shí diǎn。

我跟你約在博物館門口。

我跟你约在博物馆门口。

Wǒ gēn nǐ yuē zài bówùguǎn ménkǒu。

2. 人+對…有興趣

Examples:

我對中文有興趣。

我对中文有兴趣。

Wǒ duì Zhōngwén yǒu xìngqù。

我對打籃球有興趣。

我对打篮球有兴趣。

Wǒ duì dǎ lánqiú yǒu xìngqù。

LESSON 2

STORY

The premier is on Valentine's Day. Lin buys a Teddy bear and puts it in a gift box. He plans on giving it to Jennifer. He puts the gift in his backpack and leaves home in a good mood. To his surprise, there are so many people everywhere because of this special holiday. Many people are waiting for the bus and each bus is packed with passengers. Finally, he arrives at the movie theater and from afar sees that Jeff and Jennifer are looking for him by the entrance of the theater. He just realizes that there are 5 or 6 missed phone calls on his cellphone. Today is definitely not Lin's day.

DIALOGUE

Lin：對不起！我遲到了！

对不起！我迟到了！

Duìbùqǐ！Wǒ chídào le！

Jennifer：你怎麼那麼慢？我們等你等了半個小時了！

你怎么那么慢？我们等你等了半个小时了！

Nǐ zěnme nàme màn？Wǒmen děng nǐ děng le bàn ge xiǎoshí le！

Lin：唉！眞對不起！都是因爲我坐的車太擠了！

唉！真对不起！都是因为我坐的车太挤了！

Ai！Zhēn duìbùqǐ！Dōushì yīnwèi wǒ zuò de chē tài jǐ le！

Jeff：少來了！車太擠跟你遲到有關係嗎？

少来了！车太挤跟你迟到有关系吗？

Shǎoláile！Chē tài jǐ gēn nǐ chídào yǒu guānxī ma？

Lin：當然有！因爲人太多，所以我來不及下車！

当然有！因为人太多，所以我来不及下车！

Dāngrán yǒu！Yīnwèi rén tài duō，suǒyǐ wǒ láibùjí xià

chē！

DISCUSSION

1. Why was Lin late?
2. How long had Jenny and Jeff been waiting?

VOCABULARY

	Traditional Character	Simplified Character	Pinyin	English
1	遲到	迟到	chídào	[動] being late
2	慢	慢	màn	[形] slow
3	等	等	děng	[動] wait
4	半個小時	半个小时	bàn ge xiǎoshí	[名] half an hour
5	擠	挤	jǐ	[形] crowded
6	當然	当然	dāngrán	[副] of course; sure
7	關係	关系	guānxi	[形] related to; having to do with
8	下車	下车	xià chē	[動] get off

EXPRESSION

	Traditional Character	Simplified Character	Pinyin	English
1	唉	唉	ai	Oh
2	少來了	少来了	shǎoláile	C'mon
3	當然有	当然有	dāngrán yǒu	of course
4	來不及	来不及	láibùjí	too time

GRAMMAR

1. 怎麼那麼+adj

Examples:

怎麼那麼久？

怎么那么久？

Zěnme nàme jiǔ？

怎麼那麼辣？

怎么那么辣？

Zěnme nàme là？

2. VOV了+時間

Examples:

我等你等了半個小時。

我等你等了半个小时。

Wǒ děng nǐ děng le bàn ge xiǎoshí。

他吃飯吃了四十分鐘。

他吃饭吃了四十分钟。

Tā chī fàn chī le sì shí fēn zhōng。

3. 人+來不及+V

Examples:

我來不及下車。

我来不及下车。

Wǒ láibùjí xià chē。

我來不及吃早飯。

我来不及吃早饭。

Wǒ láibùjí chī zǎofàn。

I. PRACTICE

1.

Q：我們約在哪兒碰面？

我们约在哪儿碰面？

Wǒmen yuē zài nǎr pèngmiàn？

A：我跟你約在電影院售票口前。

我跟你约在电影院售票口前。

Wǒ gēn nǐ yuē zài diànyǐng shòupiàokǒu qián。

Practice

Q：我們約什麼時候碰面？

我们约什么时候碰面？

Wǒmen yuē shénme shíhòu pèngmiàn？

→A：＿＿＿＿＿＿＿＿＿

2.

　　Q：你等了多久？

　　　　你等了多久？

　　　　Nǐ děng le duōjiǔ？

　　A：我等了半個小時。

　　　　我等了半个小时。

　　　　Wǒ děng le bàn ge xiǎoshí。

Practice

　　　　Q：你吃了多久？

　　　　　　你吃了多久？

　　　　　　Nǐ chī le duōjiǔ？

　　　　→A：_____

3.

　　Q：公車太擠跟你遲到有關係嗎？

　　　　公交车太挤跟你迟到有关系吗？

　　　　Gōngchē tài jǐ gēn nǐ chídào yǒu guānxi ma？

　　A：當然有。

　　　　当然有。

　　　　Dāngrán yǒu。

Practice

　　　　Q：功夫跟中文有關係嗎？

　　　　　　功夫跟中文有关系吗？

　　　　　　Gōngfū gēn Zhōngwén yǒu guānxi ma？

　　　　→A：_____

4.

    Q：爲什麼Lin遲到了？

    为什么Lin迟到了？

    Wèishénme Lin chídào le？

    A：因爲他來不及下車，所以他遲到了。

    因为他来不及下车，所以他迟到了。

    Yīnwèi tā láibùjí xià chē，suǒyǐ tā chídào le。

Practice

    Q：爲什麼你學中文？

    为什么你学中文？

    Wèishénme nǐ xué Zhōngwén？

    →A：_____

II. EXERCISE

1. Complete the following dialogues

    A：我們約在哪兒碰面？

    我们约在哪儿碰面？

    Wǒmen yuē zài nǎr pèngmiàn？

    B：_____。

    A：你學中文學了多久了？

    你学中文学了多久了？

    Nǐ xué Zhōngwén xué le duōjiǔ le？

    B：_____。

A：中文跟功夫有關係嗎？

中文跟功夫有关系吗？

Zhōngwén gēn gōngfū yǒu guānxi ma？

B：＿＿＿＿＿＿＿＿＿。

A：為什麼你學中文？

为什么你学中文？

Wèishénme nǐ xué Zhōngwén？

B：因為＿＿＿＿＿，所以＿＿＿＿＿。

因为＿＿＿＿＿，所以＿＿＿＿＿。

Yīnwèi＿＿＿＿＿，suǒyǐ＿＿＿＿＿。

2. Complete the following task

    A. Role play

    In groups of two, have student A invite student B to the movies, to go shopping, to a concert, to a ball game, etc.

    B. Group task

    In groups of three to five, introduce the students to a movie made in Taiwan, Hong Kong or China. The teacher can pick a movie of his/her choice. The introduction needs to include a brief account of the story, the main characters, and a skit of the theme song.

III. SUPPLEMENTARY EXPLANATION

1. 怎麼那麼+adj 跟「為什麼」的不同之處在於除了表示疑問之外，說話者還帶有驚訝或不滿意的情緒。

The difference between "怎麼那麼+adj" and "為什麼" is that "怎麼那麼+adj", used to express doubt, can infer that the speaker is surprised or unsatisfied.

中國武術

Chinese Martial Arts	太極拳 太极拳	詠春拳 咏春拳	少林派 少林派	武當派 武当派	氣功 气功	輕功 轻功
Pinyin	tàijíquán	yǒng chūn quán	shàolínpài	wǔ dāngpài	qìgōng	qīng gōng
English	Tai chi chuan	Wing Chun	Shaolin Sect	Wudang Sect; Wu-tang clan	qigong	qinggong

IV. CULTURAL NOTES

About Kung Fu（功夫）

　　Many people are amazed by those who can master Kung Fu, especially the ones in the Chinese movies who can effortlessly hop onto a rooftop or take down much stronger opponents, unarmed. Chinese martial arts has a very long history and it is part of the Chinese culture. It is not just for attack and defense; for many learners, Chinese martial arts is a way to improve their health and mentality. The most widely known sects of Chinese Kung Fu are Tai Chi and Wing Chun. Tai Chi is a "softer" type of martial arts which emphasizes "qi" and the equilibrium of the body. Most Tai Chi learners do it for the health benefits. Wing Chun, on the other hand, emphasizes strength and speed. It is not only a kind of sports but also a combat form. Wing Chun is sometimes incorporated in military or security staff training.

What Are You Interested in?

你的興趣是什麼？

Warm Up Activities

1. What are you interested in?
2. Tell us about what you like to do in your free time.

LESSON 1

STORY

The exhibition hall downtown is now presenting a well-known fashion designer's classic collection of the decade. The designer is also there to share the concepts behind the collection. Linda does not want to miss this once-in-a-lifetime opportunity. Today, during lunch in the cafeteria, Linda invites her friends to the exhibition.

DIALOGUE

Linda： 這個週末，有一個展覽很不錯，你們要不要一
起去看？

这个周末，有一个展览很不错，你们要不要一
起去看？

Zhè ge zhōumò，yǒu yī ge zhǎnlǎn hěn búcuò，nǐmen
yàobúyào yìqǐ qù kàn？

Maria： 對不起，我想在家試做新菜。Jennifer呢？

对不起，我想在家试做新菜。Jennifer呢？

Duìbùqǐ，wǒ xiǎng zài jiā shì zuò xīn cài。Jennifer ne？

Jennifer：我也沒空，我不但要練習打拳，還要陪我媽媽
去逛街。

我也没空，我不但要练习打拳，还要陪我妈妈
去逛街。

Wǒ yě méikòng。Wǒ búdàn yào liànxí dǎquán，hái yào
péi wǒ māma qù guàngjiē。

Maria：　Linda，你要不要問Mark？

Linda，你要不要问Mark？

Linda，nǐ yàobúyào wèn Mark？

Linda：算了吧！他只對籃球跟女朋友有興趣。

算了吧！他只对篮球跟女朋友有兴趣。

Suànleba！Tā zhǐ duì lánqiú gēn nǚpéngyǒu yǒu xìngqù。

DISCUSSION

1. What is Linda doing this weekend? Is she inviting anyone?
2. What about Jennifer and Maria?

VOCABULARY

	Traditional Character	Simplified Character	Pinyin	English
1	展覽	展览	zhǎnlǎn	[名] exhibition
2	試	试	shì	[動] try
3	沒空	没空	méikòng	[形] busy; having had plans
4	陪	陪	péi	[動] accompany
5	逛街	逛街	guàngjiē	[動] shop
6	問	问	wèn	[動] ask
7	只	只	zhǐ	[副] only
8	籃球	篮球	lánqiú	[名] basketball

EXPRESSION

	Traditional Character	Simplified Character	Pinyin	English
1	算了吧	算了吧	suànleba	forget about it

GRAMMAR

1. 不但⋯還⋯

Examples:

新年晚會不但有唱歌，還有表演。

新年晚会不但有唱歌，还有表演。

Xīnnián wǎnhuì búdàn yǒu chànggē，hái yǒu biǎoyǎn。

他不但會說中文，還會說英文。

他不但会说中文，还会说英文。

Tā búdàn huì shuō Zhōngwén，hái huì shuō Yīngwén。

2. A陪B＋V

Examples:

我陪媽媽去逛街。

我陪妈妈去逛街。

Wǒ péi māma qù guàngjiē。

我陪她去看表演。

我陪她去看表演。

Wǒ péi tā qù kàn biǎoyǎn。

LESSON 2

There are so many people from the press and the media at the exhibition, taking photos with flash. Linda is excited and nervous when she sees the designer. She is recording everything with her pen and camera. When Linda passes by the refreshments, she sees Mark filling the empty glass in his hand with coke.

DIALOGUE

Linda：Mark！真巧！在這裡遇到你！

Mark！真巧！在这里遇到你！

Mark！Zhēnqiǎo！Zài zhè lǐ yùdào nǐ！

Mark：是啊！我同學得做報告，所以我陪她來看。

是啊！我同学得做报告，所以我陪她来看。

Shì a！Wǒ tóngxué děi zuò bàogào，suǒyǐ wǒ péi tā lái kàn。

Linda：那，你女朋友呢？

那，你女朋友呢？

Nà，nǐ nǚpéngyǒu ne？

Mark： 她在那邊，忙著拍照、問問題什麼的。

她在那边，忙着拍照、问问题什么的。

Tā zài nà biān，máng zhe pāizhào、wèn wèntí shénmede。

Linda： 她對藝術有興趣嗎？有空的話，我想跟她一起喝杯咖啡、聊聊天！

她对艺术有兴趣吗？有空的话，我想跟她一起喝杯咖啡、聊聊天！

Tā duì yìshù yǒu xìngqù ma？Yǒukòng dehuà，wǒ xiǎng gēn tā yìqǐ hē bēi kāfēi、liáoliáotiān！

DISCUSSION

1. Who did Linda see at the exhibition?
2. Why was Mark there?
3. Where was Mark's girlfriend?

VOCABULARY

	Traditional Character	Simplified Character	Pinyin	English
1	遇到	遇到	yùdào	[動] meet; run into
2	得	得	děi	[動] have to
3	做報告 報告	做报告 报告	zuò bàogào bàogào	[動] write a paper [名] report
4	忙著	忙着	mángzhe	[動] busy doing something
5	拍照	拍照	pāizhào	[動] take pictures
6	問題	问题	wèntí	[名] question
7	藝術	艺术	yìshù	[名] art
8	杯	杯	bēi	[量] measure word： glass
9	咖啡	咖啡	kāfēi	[名] coffee

EXPRESSION

	Traditional Character	Simplified Character	Pinyin	English
1	真巧	真巧	zhēn qiǎo	What a coincidence
2	…什麼的	…什么的	…shénmede	…and such

GRAMMAR

1. 忙著+V

Examples:

他忙著拍照。

他忙着拍照。

Tā mángzhe pāizhào。

我忙著做功課。

我忙着做功课。

Wǒ mángzhe zuò gōngkè。

2. A、B什麼的

Examples:

他忙著拍照、問問題什麼的。

他忙着拍照、问问题什么的。

Tā mángzhe pāizhào、wèn wèntí shénmede。

週末我喜歡逛街、看電影什麼的。

周末我喜欢逛街、看电影什么的。

Zhōumò wǒ xǐhuān guàngjiē、kàn diànyǐng shénmede。

3. 有空的話，我想…

Examples:

有空的話，我想跟他一起喝杯咖啡。

有空的话，我想跟他一起喝杯咖啡。

Yǒukòng dehuà，wǒ xiǎng gēn tā yìqǐ hē bēi kāfēi。

有空的話，我想去中國。

有空的话，我想去中国。

Yǒukòng dehuà，wǒ xiǎng qù Zhōngguó。

I. PRACTICE

1.

Q：你要不要一起去看？

你要不要一起去看？

Nǐ yàobúyào yìqǐ qù kàn？

A：(1) 好啊！

好啊！

Hǎo a！

(2) 對不起，我沒空。

对不起，我没空。

Duìbùqǐ，wǒ méikòng。

Practice

Q：你要不要一起去看電影？

你要不要一起去看电影？

Nǐ yàobúyào yìqǐ qù kàn diànyǐng？

→A：＿＿＿＿＿＿＿＿＿

2.

Q：你對什麼有興趣？

你对什么有兴趣？

Nǐ duì shénme yǒu xìngqù？

A：我對中文有興趣。

我对中文有兴趣。

Wǒ duì Zhōngwén yǒu xìngqù。

Practice

Q：你對什麼有興趣？

你对什么有兴趣？

Nǐ duì shénme yǒu xìngqù？

→A：＿＿＿＿＿＿＿＿＿＿＿

3.

Q：有空的話，你想做什麼？

有空的话，你想做什么？

Yǒukòng dehuà，nǐ xiǎng zuòshénme？

A：有空的話，我想去看電影。

有空的话，我想去看电影。

Yǒukòng dehuà，wǒ xiǎng qù kàn diànyǐng。

Practice

Q：有空的話，你想學什麼？

有空的话，你想学什么？

Yǒukòng dehuà，nǐ xiǎng xué shénme？

→A：＿＿＿＿＿＿＿＿＿＿＿

4.

Q：現在他做什麼？

現在他做什么？

Xiànzài tā zuò shénme？

A：他忙著拍照、問問題什麼的。

他忙着拍照、问问题什么的。

Tā mángzhe pāizhào、wèn wèntí shénmede。

Q：你早上吃了什麼？

你早上吃了什么？

Nǐ zǎoshang chī le shénme？

→A：_____

II. EXERCISE

1. Complete the following dialogues

A：你要不要一起去看電影？

你要不要一起去看电影？

Nǐ yàobúyào yìqǐ qù kàn diànyǐng？

B：_____。

A：你對什麼有興趣？

你对什么有兴趣？

Nǐ duì shénme yǒu xìngqù？

B：_____。

A：你喜歡做什麼？

你喜欢做什么？

Nǐ xǐhuān zuò shénme ?

B：＿＿＿＿＿＿＿＿＿＿。

A：有空的話，你想去哪裡玩？

有空的话，你想去哪里玩？

Yǒukòng dehuà，nǐ xiǎng qù nǎlǐ wán ?

B：＿＿＿＿＿＿＿＿＿＿。

2. Complete the following task

Have the students interview one another concerning the things they like to do and then present it before the class.

III. SUPPLEMENTARY EXPLANATION

有關展覽

Exhibition	畫展 画展	攝影展 摄影展	文物展 文物展	雕塑展 雕塑展	設計展 设计展	影展 影展
Pinyin	huàzhǎn	shèyǐngzhǎn	wén wù zhǎn	diāosù zhǎn	shèjì zhǎn	yǐngzhǎn
English	art exhibition	photography exhibition	cultural relics exhibition	sculpture Exhibition	design exhibition	movie festival

IV. CULTURAL NOTES

Euphemisms in Chinese（中國人的委婉藝術）

Euphemisms are used when you are to express something you feel too embarrassed to say directly.

First, let us talk about refusals. To avoid hurting other's feeling, we might come up with "excuses" to turn down people's invitation. For example, you can say that you have been busy or you already have something planned. You might also try to come up with an alternative plan such as asking someone else to go with the person who invited you.

In terms of use of language, the Chinese find some terms embarrassing to say and thus come up with alternative ways of expressing the same ideas. For example, instead of saying "toilet", the terms "number one" or "makeup room" are used to refer to restroom. These terms, however, do not usually appear on Chinese learning textbooks. Another example is that, when a family member passed away, the Chinese say that he or she "has left" instead of "died". A foreign student once heard that expression and asked "where has he left to?", making it a very awkward moment.

When learning a language, it is thus important to also learn its euphemisms.

第七章
UNIT 7

Let's Make Spring Rolls at My House
來我家包春捲

Warm Up Activities

1. Have you had spring rolls? Do you know how they are made?
2. Can pick a dish and introduce to us how it is made?

LESSON 1

Jennifer's grandparents are visiting New York from Shanghai and are now staying with her. Jennifer invited her friends to come over this weekend to make dumplings and spring rolls together. Her grandmother prepared many ingredients. She shows Jennifer's friends how to wrap dumplings and spring rolls. Everyone is laughing because none of them makes good ones.

DIALOGUE

Jennifer：外婆已經幫我們把材料都準備好了。

外婆已经帮我们把材料都准备好了。

Wàipó yǐjīng bāng wǒmen bǎ cáiliào dōu zhǔnbèi hǎo le。

外婆：來，我先教你們包春捲，比較容易，只要把餡兒放在春捲皮上，再捲起來就行了。

来，我先教你们包春卷，比较容易，只要把馅儿放在春卷皮上，再卷起来就行了。

Lái，wǒ xiān jiāo nǐmen bāo chūnjuǎn，bǐjiào róngyì，zhǐyào bǎ xiànr fàng zài chūnjuǎnpí shàng，zài juǎn qǐ lái jiù xíng le。

Maria：我以為只有在餐廳才吃得到春捲，沒想到自己也可以做。

我以為只有在餐廳才吃得到春卷，沒想到自己也可以做。

Wǒ yǐwéi zhǐyǒu zài cāntīng cái chīdedào chūnjuǎn，méixiǎng dào zìjǐ yě kěyǐ zuò。

Linda： 包餃子比較難，要包得好看，不太容易。

包饺子比较难，要包得好看，不太容易。

Bāo jiǎozi bǐjiào nán，yào bāo de hǎokàn，bú tài róngyì。

Mark： 是啊，看起來很簡單，可是我怎麼包都很難看。

是啊，看起来很简单，可是我怎么包都很难看。

Shì a，kànqǐlái hěn jiǎndān，kěshì wǒ zěnme bāo dōu hěn nánkàn。

DISCUSSION

1. How is a spring roll wrapped?
2. Is it hard to wrap a dumpling? Why?
3. Did Mark make good dumplings? Why?

VOCABULARY

	Traditional Character	Simplified Character	Pinyin	English
1	外婆	外婆	wàipó	[名] grandmother
2	來	來	lái	[動] come
3	已經	已经	yǐjīng	[副] already
4	把	把	bǎ	[介] a particle making the following noun as a direct object
5	放	放	fàng	[動] put
6	材料	材料	cáiliào	[名] ingredient
7	好	好	hǎo	[形] ready
8	包	包	bāo	[動] wrap
9	容易	容易	róngyì	[形] easy
10	只要	只要	zhǐyào	[副] just

	Traditional Character	Simplified Character	Pinyin	English
11	捲 捲起來	卷 卷起来	Juǎn juǎnqǐ lái	[動] roll
12	以為	以为	yǐwéi	[動] thought
13	只有	只有	zhǐyǒu	[副] only
14	才	才	cái	[副] only
15	難看	难看	nánkàn	[形] ugly

TERM

	Traditional Character	Simplified Character	Pinyin	English
1	春捲	春卷	chūnjuǎn	spring roll
2	餃子	饺子	jiǎozi	dumpling
3	餡兒	馅儿	xiànr	stuffing

EXPRESSION

	Traditional Character	Simplified Character	Pinyin	English
1	就行了	就行了	jiùxíngle	an expression used to mean that something would be ready or done after some preceding action

	Traditional Character	Simplified Character	Pinyin	English
2	吃ㄔ得ㄉㄜ到ㄉㄠ	吃得到	chīdedào	an expression used to mean when some food is available
3	沒ㄇㄟ想ㄒㄧㄤ到ㄉㄠ	没想到	méixiǎngdào	did not expect

GRAMMAR

1. 把+N+V+RC(Resultative Complement)

Examples:

把材料準備好

把材料准备好

Bǎ cáiliào zhǔnbèi hǎo

把春聯貼上

把春联贴上

Bǎ chūnlián tiē shàng

2. 把+N+V+DC(Directional Complement)

Examples:

把紙捲起來

把纸卷起来

Bǎ zhǐ juǎnqǐ lái

把毛筆拿出來

把毛笔拿出来

Bǎ máobǐ náchūlái

LESSON 2

STORY

Finally, everyone finished wrapping the spring rolls and dumplings. Jennifer is now deep-frying the spring rolls while Jeff is boiling the dumplings. Jeff is not sure if the dumplings are well cooked so he asks Jennifer to take a look. All of them are chatting in the kitchen while the food is being prepared.

DIALOGUE

Jeff： Jennifer，你幫我看看，餃子煮熟了嗎？

Jennifer，你幫我看看，餃子煮熟了嗎？

Jennifer，nǐ bāng wǒ kànkàn，jiǎozi zhǔ shóu le ma？

Maria： 我以前在中國餐廳吃的餃子都是煎的。這是我第一次吃煮的餃子。

我以前在中國餐廳吃的餃子都是煎的。這是我第一次吃煮的餃子。

Wǒ yǐqián zài Zhōngguó cāntīng chī de jiǎozi dōu shì jiān de。Zhè shì wǒ dì yī cì chī zhǔ de jiǎozi。

Jennifer： 煎的比較香，但是煮的比較好吃。

煎的比較香，但是煮的比較好吃。

Jiān de bǐjiào xiāng，dànshì zhǔ de bǐjiào hǎochī。

Lin：我比較喜歡吃炸的，所以等一下我要多吃幾根
春捲。

我比較喜歡吃炸的，所以等一下我要多吃幾根
春捲。

Wǒ bǐjiào xǐhuān chī zhá de，suǒyǐ děngyíxià wǒ yào duō
chī jǐ gēn chūnjuǎn。

Jeff：好了，你們聊了這麼久，餃子應該煮熟了。

好了，你們聊了這麼久，餃子應該煮熟了。

Hǎo le，nǐmen liáo le zhème jiǔ，jiǎozi yīnggāi zhǔ shóu
le。

DISCUSSION

1. Jeff asked Jennifer to help him with what ? Why?

2. What is the difference between the dumplings Maria had before and the ones today?

3. Which kind of dumpling does Jennifer like better ?

4. Why is Lin going to have more spring rolls ?

VOCABULARY

	Traditional Character	Simplified Character	Pinyin	English
1	煮 ㄓㄨˇ	煮	zhǔ	[動] cook
2	熟 ㄕㄨˊ	熟	shóu	[動] cooked
4	煎 ㄐㄧㄢ	煎	jiān	[動] pan-fry
5	香 ㄒㄧㄤ	香	xiāng	[形] having a pleasant smell
6	健 ㄐㄧㄢˋ 康 ㄎㄤ	健康	jiànkāng	[形] healthy
7	炸 ㄓㄚˊ	炸	zhá	[動] fry
9	多 ㄉㄨㄛ	多	duō	[副] more
11	根 ㄍㄣ	根	gēn	[量] a measure word used to count items that shape like sticks

	Traditional Character	Simplified Character	Pinyin	English
12	聊ㄌㄧㄠ	聊	liáo	[動] chat; talk
13	這ㄓㄜ麼ㄇㄜ	这么	zhème	[副] this much; to a certain degree

EXPRESSION

	Traditional Character	Simplified Character	Pinyin	English
1	等ㄉㄥ一ㄧ下ㄒㄧㄚ	等一下	děngyíxià	later
2	好ㄏㄠ了ㄌㄜ	好了	hǎo le	okay; enough of something

GRAMMAR

1. 看看+V了沒有/嗎？

Examples:

我看看熟了沒有？

我看看熟了没有？

Wǒ kànkàn shóu le méiyǒu？

請你幫我看看煮好了嗎？

请你帮我看看煮好了吗？

Qǐng nǐ bāng wǒ kànkàn zhǔ hǎo le ma？

2. 這是+N+第+NU+次+V

Examples:

這是我第一次吃春捲。

这是我第一次吃春卷。

Zhè shì wǒ dì yī cì chī chūnjuǎn。

這是她第二次去臺灣。

这是她第二次去台湾。

Zhè shì tā dì èr cì qù Táiwān。

3. 多+V+幾+NU+N

Examples:

這個地方很舒服，我想多住幾天。

这个地方很舒服，我想多住几天。

Zhège dìfang hěn shūfú，wǒ xiǎng duō zhù jǐ tiān。

他對藝術很有興趣，想多看幾個展覽再回去。

他对艺术很有兴趣，想多看几个展览再回去。

Tā duì yìshù hěn yǒu xìngqù，xiǎng duō kàn jǐ ge zhǎnlǎn zài huíqu。

I. PRACTICE

1.

Q：餃子怎麼做？

饺子怎么做？

Jiǎozi zěnme zuò？

A：把餡兒放在餃子皮裡包起來。

把馅儿放在饺子皮里包起来。

Bǎ xiànr fàng zài jiǎozipí lǐ bāo qǐ lái。

Practice

Q：你的書呢？

你的书呢？

Nǐ de shū ne？

→A：＿＿＿＿＿＿＿＿

2.

Q：這個字，你再寫一次。

这个字，你再写一次。

Zhè ge zì，nǐ zài xiě yí cì。

A：我怎麼寫都寫不好。

我怎么写都写不好。

Wǒ zěnme xiě dōu xiě bù hǎo。

Practice

Q：太極拳很難學嗎？

太极拳很难学吗？

Tàijíquán hěn nán xué ma？

→A：＿＿＿＿＿＿＿＿

3.

Q：我寫中國字寫得不好看。

我写中国字写得不好看。

Wǒ xiě Zhōngguó zì xiě de bù hǎokàn。

A：你要多練習幾次。

你要多练习几次。

Nǐ yào duō liànxí jǐ cì。

Practice

Q：我的中文，说得不好。

我的中文，说得不好。

Wǒ de Zhōngwén，shuō de bù hǎo。

→A：＿＿＿＿＿＿＿＿＿

II. EXERCISE

1. Complete the following dialogues

A：春聯寫好了，怎麼辦？

春联写好了，怎么办？

Chūnlián xiě hǎo le zěnmebàn？

B：＿＿＿＿＿＿＿＿＿＿。

A：這是你第一次來嗎？

这是你第一次来吗？

Zhè shì nǐ dì yī cì lái ma？

B：對，＿＿＿＿＿。

对，＿＿＿＿＿。

Duì，＿＿＿＿＿。

A：餃子沒煮熟，怎麼辦？

饺子没煮熟，怎么办？

Jiǎozi méi zhǔ shóu，zěnmebàn？

B：你要多＿＿＿＿＿。

你要多＿＿＿＿＿。

Nǐ yào duō＿＿＿＿＿。

2. Complete the following task

A. Tell us how a spring roll is made with the help of the picture(s).

B. Pick a dish you like and introduce to the class how it is made.

III. SUPPLEMENTARY EXPLANATION

烹調方法

cooking	煎 煎	煮 煮	炒 炒	炸 炸	蒸 蒸	滷 卤	烤 烤	紅燒 红烧
Pinyin	jiān	zhǔ	chǎo	zhá	zhēng	lǔ	kǎo	hóngshāo
English	pan-fry	cook; boil	saute; stir-fry	fry	steam	stew	grill	braise in brown sauce

口味

taste	酸 酸	甜 甜	苦 苦	辣 辣	鹹 咸	麻 麻	淡 淡	濃 浓
Pinyin	suān	tián	kǔ	là	xián	má	dàn	nóng
English	sour	sweet	bitter	hot; spicy	salty	numbing	mild; light	thick; rich

菜名

menu	宮保雞丁 宫保鸡丁	清炒蝦仁 清炒虾仁	北京烤鴨 北京烤鸭	麻婆豆腐 麻婆豆腐	紅燒牛肉麵 红烧牛肉面
Pinyin	Gōng bǎo jī dīng	Qīng chǎo xiā rén	Běi jīng kǎo yā	Má pó dòu fǔ	Hóng shāo niú ròu miàn
English	Kung pao chicken	Sauteed shrimp	Peking duck	Hot and spicy tofu	Braised beef noodle soup

IV. CULTURAL NOTES

Eight Regional Cuisines in China（中國最有名的八大菜系）

The eight most distinctive regional cuisines in China are Chuan, Yue, Lu, Su, Zhe, Xiang, Min, and Hui. Chuan cuisine, short for Sichuan, has been made famous by dishes common to Chengdu and Chongqing. Sichuanese food is characterized by a brand of sour and spice that numbs the mouth, the excessive use of oil, and its richness in taste. Yue cuisine denotes Cantonese food. Hong Kong has long been an international trading hub and its food has thus been influenced by western cuisine. Yue food is colorful, oily, and smooth in texture without being too greasy. Su cuisine refers to food from the Jiangsu province, which is known for being salty and sweet and having a mellow taste. Zhe dishes, meaning from Zhejiang, are served in small portions and are very refined, characterized by a fresh flavor and a crunchy yet chewy texture. Xiang, also known as Hunan cuisine, is famous for being spicy and exquisite, employing more than ten different cutting techniques, such as julienning, dicing, and mincing. Min cuisine refers to that from southern Fujian. Fujian is on the southeastern coast of China and it goes without saying that seafood is a common ingredient in Min cuisine. Hui cuisine is mostly comprised of Huizhou dishes from Anhui. As Anhui is an inland province, its dishes are known for including wild plants and animals as ingredients. Taiwan is home to immigrants from all eight places; as such, this island garners all flavors and presents them in full.

Chinese Dining Etiquette（華人吃飯的禮節）

1. Seating arrangement: the seat that faces the door is the seat of honor, and thus reserved for the guest of honor. The youngest person should be seated adjacent to the door, which is a place that is also usually reserved for the host. In the event that you are not sure where to be seated, wait for the host to make arrangements.

2. Do not rummage through the dishes or point at people with your chopsticks. Also, do not leave your chopsticks sticking upright out of the rice in your bowl. Remember not to go under other people's chopsticks when you are reaching for food.

3. According to Chinese tradition, sharing dishes, retrieving food from a common plate typifies a bond between those that are dining together. However, in light of health concerns, Chinese restaurants now provide serving spoons and chopsticks.

4. Sit up when you dine. Hold your bowl with one of your hands and keep it near your mouth. Do not slouch or bow your head close to the table to reach the bowl. Do not slurp when having soup.

Go, Mark! Go!
一起幫Mark加油！

Warm Up Activities

1. What is your favorite sport? Why?
2. What kind of ball game do you like to watch? Why?

LESSON 1

STORY

College basketball season is going to start next month! Last year, we lost by only one point. This season, there is a two-week training before the game starts. That explains why Mark and Lin are not around recently. Jennifer and Jeff join Maria and Linda at the cafeteria during lunch and talk about the basketball season this year.

DIALOGUE

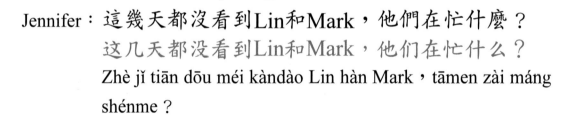

Jennifer：這幾天都沒看到Lin和Mark，他們在忙什麼？
这几天都没看到Lin和Mark，他们在忙什么？
Zhè jǐ tiān dōu méi kàndào Lin hàn Mark，tāmen zài máng shénme？

Linda：下星期就要籃球比賽了，他們正在加緊練習！
下星期就要篮球比赛了，他们正在加紧练习！
Xià xīngqí jiù yào lánqiú bǐsài le，tāmen zhèngzài jiājǐn liànxí！

Maria：去年差一點就得到冠軍，真是太可惜了。
去年差一点就得到冠军，真是太可惜了。
Qùnián chā yī diǎn jiù dédào guànjūn，zhēnshì tài kěxí le。

Jeff：是啊，本來我們贏兩分，最後一秒鐘，他們投
　　　進了一個三分球，後來輸了一分。

　　　是啊，本来我们赢兩分，最后一秒钟，他们投
　　　进了一个三分球，后来输了一分。

　　　Shì a，běnlái wǒmen yíng liǎn fēn，zuìhòu yī miǎozhōng，
　　　tāmen tóujìn le yí ge sānfēnqiú，hòulái shū le yì fēn。

Linda：那真是一場緊張的比賽。

　　　　那真是一场紧张的比赛。

　　　　Nà zhēnshì yì chǎng jǐnzhāng de bǐsài。

DISCUSSION

1. Why are Mark and Lin not around recently?

2. What was the result of the basketball game last year?

VOCABULARY

	Traditional Character	Simplified Character	Pinyin	English
1	忙	忙	máng	[形] busy
2	比賽	比赛	bǐsài	[名/動] game (n.) play (v.)
3	正在	正在	zhèngzài	[副] an adverb used to express an ongoing action
4	加緊	加紧	jiājǐn	[動] hurry to do some- thing; more often to do something
5	得到	得到	dédào	[動] obtain; get
6	本來	本来	běnlái	[副] originally
7	贏	赢	yíng	[動] win
8	分	分	fēn	[名] point; score
9	一秒鐘	一秒钟	yì miǎozhōng	[名] one second
10	投進	投进	tóujìn	[動] shoot in

	Traditional Character	Simplified Character	Pinyin	English
11	後來	后来	hòulái	[副] afterwards
12	輸	输	shū	[動] lose
13	場	场	chǎng	[量] a measure word used to count the number of sporting activities
14	緊張	紧张	jǐnzhāng	[形] nervous

TERM

	Traditional Character	Simplified Character	Pinyin	English
1	冠軍	冠军	guànjūn	champion; championship
2	三分球	三分球	sānfēnqiú	three pointer

EXPRESSION

	Traditional Character	Simplified Character	Pinyin	English
1	這幾天	这几天	zhè jǐ tiān	recently; these days
2	就要…了	就要…了	jiùyào…le	an expression used to mean when something is about to happen
3	差一點就	差一点就	chāyìdiǎn jiù	an expression used to mean when something almost happened

GRAMMAR

1. 就要+V+了

Examples:

他明天就要回上海了。

他明天就要回上海了。

Tā míngtiān jiùyào huí Shànghǎi le。

下星期就要比賽了。

下星期就要比赛了。

Xià xīngqí jiùyào bǐsài le。

2. 差一點就+V+了

Examples:

我們差一點就贏了，可是最後輸了。

我们差一点就赢了，可是最后输了。

Wǒmen chāyìdiǎn jiù yíng le，kěshì zuìhòu shū le。

我昨天差一點就趕上那一場電影了。

我昨天差一点就赶上那一场电影了。

Wǒ zuótiān chāyìdiǎn jiù gǎnshàng nà yì chǎng diànyǐng le。

3. 本來+V，後來+V+了。

Examples:

我本來不會說中文，後來會了。

我本来不会说中文，后来会了。

Wǒ běnlái búhuì shuō Zhōngwén，hòulái huì le。

他本來不喜歡籃球，後來喜歡了。

他本来不喜欢篮球，后来喜欢了。

Tā běnlái bù xǐhuān lánqiú，hòulái xǐhuān le。

LESSON 2

STORY

In the locker room of the gym, Linda and Maria are changing for the practicing session in the afternoon. The cheerleaders have come up with a new performance for the tournament this year. They plan on doing a lot of leapings and flippings to encourage the basketball team. Maria tells Linda that she had been eating too much during the winter and that she has to start excersicing to get back in shape orelse she would not be able to do any of the tricks.

DIALOGUE

Maria：最近吃太多，胖了五磅，這件衣服快要穿不下了。

最近吃太多，胖了五磅，这件衣服快要穿不下了。

Zuìjìn chī tài duō，pàng le wǔ bàng，zhè jiàn yīfú kuàiyào chuān búxià le。

Linda：我也是，雖然天天運動，可是也不會瘦。

我也是，虽然天天运动，可是也不会瘦。

Wǒ yěshì，suīrán tiāntiān yùndòng，kěshì yě búhuì shòu。

Maria： 這次的動作比較難，跳得好累。

這次的动作比较难，跳得好累。

Zhè cì de dòngzuò bǐjiào nán，tiào de hǎo lèi。

Linda： 嗯，好幾個動作，我一直學不會。

嗯，好几个动作，我一直学不会。

En，hǎo jǐ ge dòngzuò，wǒ yìzhí xué búhuì。

Maria： 我們一起加油！

我们一起加油！

Wǒmen yìqǐ jiāyóu！

DISCUSSION

1. What does Maria worry about?
2. Does Linda worry about the same thing?
3. What about the moves in the performance this year?

VOCABULARY

	Traditional Character	Simplified Character	Pinyin	English
1	胖	胖	pàng	[形] overweight
2	磅	磅	bàng	[量] pound
3	衣-服	衣服	yīfu	[名] clothing; top
4	穿	穿	chuān	[動] wear
5	雖然	虽然	suīrán	[連] although
6	天天	天天	tiāntiān	[名] everyday
7	運動	运动	yùndòng	[動] exercise
8	會	会	huì	[動] can (to be able to)
9	瘦	瘦	shòu	[形] slim; skinny
10	次	次	cì	[量] a measure word used to count numerated events (time)

	Traditional Character	Simplified Character	Pinyin	English
11	動作	动作	dòngzuò	[名] move
12	跳	跳	tiào	[動] jump; leap
13	累	累	lèi	[形] tired; tiring
14	嗯	嗯	en	[助] oh

EXPRESSION

	Traditional Character	Simplified Character	Pinyin	English
1	穿不下	穿不下	chuān búxià	(clothing) does not fit (because the size is too small)
2	我也是	我也是	wǒ yěshì	same with me; I am with you
3	好幾個	好几个	hǎo jǐ ge	many
4	學不會	学不会	xué búhuì	not able to understand after learning; not able to master something after practicing
5	加油	加油	jiāyóu	Go! (used as pep talk)

GRAMMAR

1. V+不下

Examples:

這衣服太小，我穿不下。

这衣服太小，我穿不下。

Zhè yīfu tài xiǎo，wǒ chuān búxià。

我吃不下。

我吃不下。

Wǒ chī búxià。

2. 雖然…可是…

Examples:

雖然很難，可是我一定可以學會。

虽然很难，可是我一定可以学会。

Suīrán hěn nán，kěshì wǒ yídìng kěyǐ xuéhuì。

他雖然沒練習，可是跳得很好。

他虽然没练习，可是跳得很好。

Tā suīrán méi liànxí，kěshì tiào de hěn hǎo。

I. PRACTICE

1.

Q：Jennifer什麼時候來？

Jennifer什么时候来？

Jennifer shénme shíhòu lái？

A：她馬上就要來了。

她马上就要来了。

Tā mǎshàng jiùyào lái le。

Practice

Q：你什麼時候回家？

你什么时候回家？

Nǐ shénme shíhòu huíjiā？

→A：＿＿＿＿＿＿＿＿＿

2.

Q：這件衣服大小合適嗎？

这件衣服大小合适吗？

Zhè jiàn yīfu dàxiǎo héshì ma？

A：太小了，我穿不下。

太小了，我穿不下。

Tài xiǎo le，wǒ chuān búxià。

Practice

Q：還要再點一個菜嗎？

还要再点一个菜吗？

Háiyào zài diǎn yí ge cài ma？

→A：＿＿＿＿＿＿＿＿＿

3.

Q：你怎麼沒去上海？

你怎么没去上海？

Nǐ zěnme méi qù Shànghǎi？

A：我本來打算去上海，後來決定去臺灣了。

我本来打算去上海，后来决定去台湾了。

Wǒ běnlái dǎsuàn qù Shànghǎi，hòulái juédìng qù Táiwān le。

Practice

Q：你會包餃子嗎？

你会包饺子吗？

Nǐ huì bāo jiǎozi ma？

→A：＿＿＿＿＿＿＿＿＿

II. EXERCISE

1. Complete the following dialogues

A：你爲什麼沒買那件衣服？

你为什么没买那件衣服？

Nǐ wèishénme méi mǎi nà jiàn yīfu？

B：＿＿＿＿＿＿＿＿＿。

A：這次比賽，誰贏了？

这次比赛，谁赢了？

Zhècì bǐsài，shéi yíng le？

B：本來＿＿＿＿，後來＿＿＿＿。

本来＿＿＿＿，后来＿＿＿＿。

Běnlái＿＿＿＿，hòulái＿＿＿＿。

2. Complete the following task

A. Introduce to the class a sports team or an athlete you like.

B. Tell the class about the result of a recent sports game you enjoyed watching.

III. SUPPLEMENTARY EXPLANATION

運動

sports	棒球 棒球	網球 网球	足球 足球	乒乓球 乒乓球	橄欖球 橄榄球	排球 排球	游泳 游泳
Pinyin	bàngqiú	wǎngqiú	zúqiú	pīngpāngqiú	gǎnlǎnqiú	páiqiú	yóuyǒng
English	baseball	tennis	soccer	ping pong; table tennis	football	volley- ball	swimming

sports	健行 健行	慢跑 慢跑	登山 登山	瑜伽 瑜伽	跳繩 跳绳	滑雪 滑雪	打太極拳 打太极拳	騎腳踏車 骑脚踏车
Pinyin	jiàn xíng	màn pǎo	dēng shān	yújiā	tiào shéng	huáxuě	dǎ tàijíquán	qí jiǎtàchē
English	hiking; power walk	jogging	moun- tain climbing	yoga	jumping rope	skiing	Tai Chi	biking

IV. CULTURAL NOTES

Eastern and Western Attitudes Toward Sport（中西方對運動的看法差異）

Traditionally speaking the Chinese view sport (yùndòng, 運動) in terms of exercise, primarily as a means of staying physically fit and preserving health. In fact, they consider over-exertion in sport as counter to maintaining good physical condition. The second character in sport, dòng (動), refers to the movement of one's extremities, and the first character, yùn (運), to the corresponding stimulation of one's internal organs. Since ancient times dòng (動) and yùn

(運) have been considered interdependent and inseparable, with the working of vitals contingent upon movement of the body and its limbs. Conversely, exterior movement can only be completed with the help of healthy internal organs.

The western world defines sport with an emphasis on competition. It is a physical challenge with the opponent being one's self, other people, or even Mother Nature. The goal is to increase physical agility and skill, having fun in the meantime and enjoying the pleasures that come along with sport.

第九章
UNIT 9

Do You Want to Apply for the Student Exchange Program?

你想申請交換計畫嗎？

Warm Up Activities

1. Do you want to apply for any student exchange program?
2. Do you know what types of documents are needed?

LESSON 1

STORY

Linda wants to learn Chinese in China or Taiwan in the coming semester. She is going to the office to learn about detailed application requirements. Jeff happens to just have come out of the office.

DIALOGUE

Jeff：嗨！Linda，你怎麼在這兒？有事嗎？
嗨！Linda，你怎么在这儿？有事吗？
Hāi！Linda，nǐ zěnme zài zhèr？Yǒu shì ma？

Linda：我有一些關於交換計畫的問題，問誰好呢？
我有一些关于交换计划的问题，问谁好呢？
Wǒ yǒu yìxiē guānyú jiāohuàn jìhuà de wèntí，wèn shéi hǎo ne？

Jeff：你是要問怎麼申請嗎？
你是要问怎么申请吗？
Nǐ shì yào wèn zěnme shēnqǐng ma？

Linda：不是，我想知道的是怎麼算學分、怎麼選課？
有沒有獎學金？

不是，我想知道的是怎么算学分、怎么选课？
有没有奖学金？

Bù shì，wǒ xiǎng zhīdào de shì zěnme suàn xuéfēn、
zěnme xuǎn kè？Yǒuméiyǒu jiǎngxuéjīn？

Jeff：喔！每個學校的要求都不一樣，你找祕書吧！
他最清楚。祝你好運！

喔！每个学校的要求都不一样，你找祕书吧！
他最清楚。祝你好运！

O！Měi ge xuéxiào de yāoqiú dōu bùyíyàng，nǐ zhǎo
mìshū ba！Tā zuì qīngchǔ。Zhù nǐ hǎoyùn！

DISCUSSION

1. What kinds of questions does Linda have?
2. Is Linda asking about the process for applying or other types of questions?
3. What is Jeff's suggestion?

VOCABULARY

	Traditional Character	Simplified Character	Pinyin	English
1	嗨	嗨	hài	[介] hi
2	有事	有事	yǒushì	[動] something come up
3	一些	一些	yìxiē	[量] some
4	關於	关于	guānyú	[介] about
5	交換計畫	交换计划	jiāohuàn jìhuà	[名] exchange program
6	申請	申请	shēnqǐng	[動] apply
7	算	算	suàn	[動] calculate
8	學分	学分	xuéfēn	[名] credit
9	選課	选课	xuǎn kè	[動] enroll (in class)
10	獎學金	奖学金	jiǎngxuéjīn	[名] scholarship

	Traditional Character	Simplified Character	Pinyin	English
11	祕書	祕書	mìshū	[名] secretary
12	學校	学校	xuéxiào	[名] school
13	要求	要求	yāoqiú	[名] requirement
14	清楚	清楚	qīngchǔ	[形] clear
15	找	找	zhǎo	[動] find

EXPRESSION

	Traditional Character	Simplified Character	Pinyin	English
1	祝你好運	祝你好运	zhù nǐ hǎoyùn	Good luck

GRAMMAR

1. 關於+…的問題，…

Examples:

關於交換計畫的問題，我應該問誰？

关于交换计划的问题，我应该问谁？

Guānyú jiāohuàn jìhuà de wèntí，wǒ yīnggāi wèn shéi？

關於你的問題，可以找祕書。

关于你的问题，可以找祕书。

Guānyú nǐ de wèntí，kěyǐ zhǎo mìshū。

2. 每+量+N1的N2都不一樣

Examples:

每個學校的要求都不一樣。

每个学校的要求都不一样。

Měi ge xuéxiào de yāoqiú dōu bùyíyàng。

每個人的興趣都不一樣。

每个人的兴趣都不一样。

Měi ge rén de xìng qù dōu bùyíyàng。

LESSON 2

STORY

Jeff is applying for the student exchange program and plans on studying at a high school in Taipei in the next semester. He will need a recommendation letter from a teacher.

DIALOGUE

Jeff： 陳老師，謝謝您幫我寫推薦信。

陈老师，谢谢您帮我写推荐信。

Chén lǎoshī，xièxie nín bāng wǒ xiě tuījiànxìn。

Ms. Chen： 不客氣！自傳、讀書計畫還有成績單什麼的，你都準備好了嗎？

不客气！自传、读书计划还有成绩单什么的，你都准备好了吗？

Búkèqì！Zìzhuàn、dúshū jìhuà háiyǒu chéngjīdān shénme de，nǐ dōu zhǔnbèi hǎo le ma？

Jeff： 都準備好了。陳老師，去臺灣留學，有什麼我應該特別注意的？

都准备好了。陈老师，去台湾留学，有什么我应该特别注意的？

Dōu zhǔnbèi hǎo le。Chén lǎoshī，qù Táiwān liúxué，yǒu shénme wǒ yīnggāi tèbié zhùyì de？

Ms. Chen：不管是食物、天氣還是文化，都跟美國不一樣，都要注意，最重要的是入境隨俗。
不管是食物、天气还是文化，都跟美国不一样，都要注意，最重要的是入境随俗。
Bùguǎn shì shíwù、tiānqì háishì wénhuà，dōu gēn Měiguó bùyíyàng，dōu yào zhùyì，zuì zhòngyào de shì Rùjìngsuísú。

Jeff：好，不管怎麼樣，我都會想辦法適應的！
好，不管怎么样，我都会想办法适应的！
Hǎo，bùguǎn zěnmeyàng，wǒ dōu huì xiǎngbànfǎ shìyìng de！

DISCUSSION

1. What did Jeff ask Chen to help with?
2. What question did Jeff ask? What did Chen say?

VOCABULARY

	Traditional Character	Simplified Character	Pinyin	English
1	推薦信	推荐信	tuījiànxìn	[名] recommendation letter
2	自傳	自传	zìzhuàn	[名] autobiography; personal statement
3	讀書計畫	读书计划	dúshū jìhuà	[名] statement of purpose; study plan
4	成績單	成绩单	chéngjīdān	[名] transcript
5	留學	留学	liúxué	[動] study overseas; study abroad
6	注意	注意	zhùyì	[動] be careful
7	食物	食物	shíwù	[名] food
8	天氣	天气	tiānqì	[名] weather
9	文化	文化	wénhuà	[名] culture
10	重要	重要	zhòngyào	[形] important
11	適應	适应	shìyìng	[動] adapt to; fit in

EXPRESSION

	Traditional Character	Simplified Character	Pinyin	English
1	入境隨俗	入境随俗	Rùjìngsuísú	do as the natives do
2	想辦法	想办法	xiǎng bànfǎ	try to ; attempt to

GRAMMAR

1. 不管A還是B，都⋯

Examples:

不管食物還是天氣，都跟美國不一樣。

不管食物还是天气，都跟美国不一样。

Bùguǎn shíwù háishì tiānqì，dōu gēn Měiguó bùyíyàng。

不管考試還是報告，都很難。

不管考试还是报告，都很难。

Bùguǎn kǎoshì háishì bàogào，dōu hěn nán。

2. 不管怎麼樣，人都⋯

Examples:

不管怎麼樣，我都會想辦法適應。

不管怎么样，我都会想办法适应。

Bùguǎn zěnmeyàng，wǒ dōu huì xiǎngbànfǎ shìyìng。

不管怎麼樣，我都要去留學。

不管怎么样，我都要去留学。

Bùguǎn zěnmeyàng，wǒ dōu yào qù liúxué。

I. PRACTICE

1.

Q：關於申請計畫，大家有問題嗎？

關于申请计划，大家有问题吗？

Guānyú shēnqǐng jìhuà，dà jiā yǒu wèn tí ma？

A：請問，學分怎麼算？

请问，学分怎么算？

Qǐngwèn，xuéfēn zěnme suàn？

Practice

Q：關於期末考試，大家有問題嗎？

关于期末考试，大家有问题吗？

Guānyú qímò kǎoshì，dàjiā yǒu wèntí ma？

→A： _____

2.

Q：我有申請計畫的問題，問誰好呢？

我有申请计划的问题，问谁好呢？

Wǒ yǒu shēnqǐng jìhuà de wèntí，wèn shéi hǎo ne？

A：你找祕書吧！他最清楚。

你找祕書吧！他最清楚。

Nǐ zhǎo mìshū ba！Tā zuì qīngchǔ。

Practice

Q：我想知道哪兒有好吃的中國菜，問誰好呢？

我想知道哪儿有好吃的中国菜，问谁好呢？

Wǒ xiǎng zhīdào nǎr yǒu hǎochī de Zhōngguó cài，wèn shéi hǎo ne？

→A：＿＿＿＿＿＿＿＿

3.

Q：有什麼我應該注意的？

有什么我应该注意的？

Yǒu shénme wǒ yīnggāi zhùyì de？

A：不管是食物還是天氣，都要注意。

不管是食物还是天气，都要注意。

Bùguǎn shì shíwù háishì tiānqì，dōu yào zhùyì。

Practice

Q：你喜歡考試還是報告？

你喜欢考试还是报告？

Nǐ xǐhuān kǎoshì háishì bàogào？

→A：＿＿＿＿＿＿＿＿

II. EXERCISE

1. Complete the following dialogues

A：我想知道哪兒有好吃的餃子，問誰好呢？

我想知道哪儿有好吃的饺子，问谁好呢？

Wǒ xiǎng zhīdào nǎr yǒu hǎo chī de jiǎozi，wèn shéi hǎo ne？

B：＿＿＿＿＿＿＿＿。

A：你喜歡唱歌還是看表演？

你喜欢唱歌还是看表演？

Nǐ xǐhuān chànggē hái shì kàn biǎoyǎn？

B：不管＿＿＿＿＿＿。

不管＿＿＿＿＿＿。

Bùguan＿＿＿＿＿＿。

2. Complete the following task

Have the students go online and search for student exchange programs. Ask them which school they would like to apply for and what are the required documents.

III. SUPPLEMENTARY EXPLANATION

學校相關詞彙

About School	註冊 注冊	學費 学费	住宿 住宿	必修 必修	選修 选修	繳費 缴费
Pinyin	zhùcè	xuéfèi	zhùsù	bìxiū	xuǎnxiū	jiǎofèi
English	register	tuition	student housing	required course; compulsory course	elective course	pay

IV. CULTURAL NOTES

Introducing Taiwan（臺灣簡介）：

Taiwan is situated on the western shore of the Pacific ocean to the southeast of China, with Japan to the north and the Philippines to the south. Taiwan is a great travel destination as it is warm year round and has sultry summers. With a total land area of 36,000 km^2, and a population of 23 million, Taiwan is not especially large, but it is rich in natural resources and boasts a diverse culture. Taiwan's topography is complex, among its features are tall mountains, plains, basins, and offshore islands. There are ecosystems representing tropical, subtropical, and temperate climes, and the tallest mountain, Jade Mountain, reaches heights of 3,952 meters (13,000 feet).

In Taiwan, you can find the social and cultural diversity in humanities. The island shares an official language with China, Mandarin Chinese, and dialects such as Hokkien and Hakka are common. Different people groups bring different cultural pockets of the island together, whether it is religious beliefs, architecture, customs, or food, all blend together in a colorful eclectic mix. Indeed food deserves special mention as authentic Japan, Thailand, Korea, and Vietnam cuisine can all be found all around the island. Foreign fare is common – there is a feast to be had for all.

Let's Go to the Theme Park!

我們去遊樂園吧！

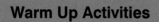
Warm Up Activities

1. What kind of plans do you usually make for holidays?
2. What are some of the recreational places around your city? Do you like theme parks? Why?

LESSON 1

STORY

Mark and Lin have been missing the Kung Fu club practice sessions. Jennifer and Jeff are planning on having outdoor activities when the weather is nice, and they are inviting Mark and Lin. Maria joins the discussion. Finally, they decide on going to the theme park.

DIALOGUE

Jennifer：春暖花開的季節，我們去郊外走走吧！

春暖花开的季节，我们去郊外走走吧！

Chūnnuǎnhuākāi de jìjié，wǒmen qù jiāowài zǒuzǒu ba！

Jeff：好主意，很久沒去遊樂場玩了，很想念坐雲霄飛車的刺激感。

好主意，很久没去游乐场玩了，很想念坐云霄飞车的刺激感。

Hǎo zhǔyì，hěn jiǔ méi qù yóulèchǎng wán le，hěn xiǎngniàn zuò Yúnxiāofēichē de cìjīgǎn。

Mark：就是啊，前一陣子為了籃球比賽緊張死了。

就是啊，前一阵子为了篮球比赛紧张死了。

Jiùshìa，qián yízhènzi wèile lánqiú bǐsài jǐnzhāng sǐle。

Lin： 趁這個週末，我們好好地放鬆一下。

趁这个周末，我们好好地放松一下。

Chèn zhè ge zhōumò，wǒmen hǎohǎode fàngsōng yíxià。

Maria： 就這麼說定了，那我來安排去遊樂場的行程。

就这么说定了，那我来安排去游乐场的行程。

Jiù zhème shuōdìng le，nà wǒ lái ānpái qù yóulèchǎng de
xíngchéng。

DISCUSSION

1. Where do Jennifer and her friends plan on going out to? When?

2. Why are they going to the theme park?

VOCABULARY

	Traditional Character	Simplified Character	Pinyin	English
1	季節	季节	jìjié	[名] season
2	郊外	郊外	jiāowài	[名] suburb
3	想念	想念	xiǎngniàn	[動] miss
4	刺激	刺激	cìjī	[名] excite
5	…感	…感	…gǎn	[名] sense (of)
6	一陣子	一阵子	yízhènzi	[名] a while
7	為了	为了	wèile	[介] for
8	趁	趁	chèn	[介] when; during
9	假期	假期	jiàqí	[名] vacation
10	好好地	好好地	hǎohǎode	[副] well; properly
11	放鬆	放松	fàngsōng	[動] relax

	Traditional Character	Simplified Character	Pinyin	English
12	安排	安排	ānpái	[動] arrange
13	行程	行程	xíngchéng	[名] plan; schedule

TERM

	Traditional Character	Simplified Character	Pinyin	English
1	遊樂場	游乐场	yóulèchǎng	theme park
2	雲霄飛車	云霄飞车	Yúnxiāofēichē	rollercoaster
3	復活節	复活节	Fùhuójié	Easter

EXPRESSION

	Traditional Character	Simplified Character	Pinyin	English
1	春暖花開	春暖花开	Chūnnuǎnhuākāi	flowers blossom as it turns warm in the spring
2	好主意	好主意	hǎo zhǔyì	good idea
3	前一陣子	前一阵子	qián yízhènzi	a while ago
4	就是啊	就是啊	jiùshì a	I know Exactly
5	放鬆一下	放松一下	fàngsōng yíxià	relax for a while
6	就這麼說定了	就这么说定了	jiù zhème shuōdìng le	Done deal

GRAMMAR

1. 爲了…

Examples:

我去臺灣是爲了學中文。

我去台湾是为了学中文。

Wǒ qù Táiwān shì wèile xué Zhōngwén。

他爲了籃球比賽練習了很久。

他为了篮球比赛练习了很久。

Tā wèile lánqiú bǐsài liànxí le hěn jiǔ。

2. Adj+死了

Examples:

我緊張死了。

我紧张死了。

Wǒ jǐnzhāng sǐle。

我累死了。

我累死了。

Wǒ lèi sǐle。

3. 趁…

Examples:

趁寒假的時候，去臺灣玩。

趁寒假的时候，去台湾玩。

Chèn hánjià de shíhòu，qù Táiwān wán。

趁天氣好出去走走。

趁天气好出去走走。

Chèn tiānqì hǎo chūqù zǒuzǒu。

LESSON 2

STORY

The weather today is perfect for an outing. The group of people take the metro to the theme park and hear screamings already when they get off. Everyone is having a good time. During noon time, they get hotdogs, pizzas, and coke for picnic.

DIALOGUE

Jeff： 排了半個鐘頭的隊，才坐到雲霄飛車，五分鐘就結束了！

排了半个钟头的队，才坐到云霄飞车，五分钟就结束了！

Pái le bàn ge zhōngtou de duì，cái zuòdào Yúnxiāofēichē，wǔ fēnzhōng jiù jiéshù le！

Mark： 別抱怨了，我們趕快再去玩別的！

别抱怨了，我们赶快再去玩别的！

Bié bàoyuàn le，wǒmen gǎnkuài zài qù wán bié de！

Maria： 剛剛嚇死我了！Jenniffer，你還好嗎？怎麼臉色發白。

刚刚吓死我了！Jenniffer，你还好吗？怎么脸色发白。

Gānggāng xiàsǐ wǒ le！Jennifer，nǐ hái hǎo ma？Zěnme liǎnsè fābái。

Jenniffer： 別管我，我想吐，讓我休息一下，你們去玩吧。

別管我，我想吐，让我休息一下，你们去玩吧。

Bié guǎn wǒ，wǒ xiǎng tù，ràng wǒ xiūxí yíxià，nǐmen qù wán ba。

Lin： 反正也快中午了，我們就休息休息吃中飯吧。

反正也快中午了，我们就休息休息吃中饭吧。

Fǎnzhèng yě kuài zhōngwǔ le，wǒmen jiù xiūxí xiūxí chī zhōngfàn ba。

DISCUSSION

1. Why was Jeff complaining?
2. What happened to Jenniffer?

VOCABULARY

	Traditional Character	Simplified Character	Pinyin	English
1	排隊	排队	páiduì	[動] line up; queue
2	半	半	bàn	[名] helf
3	鐘頭	钟头	zhōngtou	[名] hour
4	才	才	cái	[副] not…until
5	分鐘	分钟	fēnzhōng	[名] minute
6	結束	结束	jiéshù	[動] end
7	別	別	bié	[副] do not
8	抱怨	抱怨	bàoyuàn	[動] complain
9	趕快	赶快	gǎnkuài	[副] hurry
10	別的	別的	biéde	[名] other things
11	剛剛	刚刚	gānggāng	[副] just then
12	嚇	吓	xià	[動] scare; frighten

	Traditional Character	Simplified Character	Pinyin	English
13	臉色	脸色	liǎnsè	[名] complexion
14	發白	发白	fābái	[動] turn pal; turn white
15	吐	吐	tù	[動] vomit; throw up
16	反正	反正	fǎnzhèng	[副] anyway
17	中飯 晚飯 早飯	中饭 晚饭 早饭	zhōngfàn wǎnfàn zǎofàn	[名] lunch dinner breakfast

EXPRESSION

	Traditional Character	Simplified Character	Pinyin	English
1	嚇死我了	吓死我了	xiàsǐ wǒ le	I am scared to death
2	你還好嗎？	你还好吗？	nǐ hái hǎo ma	Are you okay?
3	別管我	别管我	bié guǎn wǒ	Leave me alone

GRAMMAR

1. V+Time Spent+才+V+

Examples:

我排了半個鐘頭才坐到雲霄飛車。

我排了半个钟头才坐到云霄飞车。

Wǒ pái le bàn ge zhōngtou cái zuòdào Yúnxiāofēichē。

他學了半年才學會。

他学了半年才学会。

Tā xué le bànnián cái xuéhuì。

2. V+Time Spent 就+

Examples:

你走五分鐘就到了。

你走五分钟就到了。

Nǐ zǒu wǔ fēnzhōng jiù dào le。

我看了一個鐘頭就看完了。

我看了一个钟头就看完了。

Wǒ kàn le yí ge zhōngtou jiù kànwán le。

I. PRACTICE

1.

Q：你爲什麼學太極拳？

你为什么学太极拳？

Nǐ wèishénme xué tàijíquán？

A：我爲了健康學太極拳。

我为了健康学太极拳。

Wǒ wèile jiànkāng xué tàijíquán。

Practice

Q： 你爲什麼學中文？

你为什么学中文？

Nǐ wèishénme xué Zhōngwén？

→A： _____

2.

Q：你等了很久嗎？

你等了很久吗？

Nǐ děng le hěn jiǔ ma？

A：

1.是啊，我等了半個鐘頭，他才來。

是啊，我等了半个钟头，他才来。

Shì a，wǒ děng le bàn ge zhōngtou，tā cái lái。

2.不，我等了五分鐘，他就來了。

不，我等了五分钟，他就来了。

Bù，wǒ děng le wǔ fēnzhōng，tā jiù lái le。

Practice

Q：你看了很久，才看完嗎？

你看了很久，才看完吗？

Nǐ kàn le hěn jiǔ，cái kànwán ma？

→A：＿＿＿＿＿＿＿＿＿

3.

Q：你打算什麼時候去旅行？

你打算什么时候去旅行？

Nǐ dǎsuàn shénme shíhòu qù lǚxíng？

A：我打算趁寒假的時候去旅行。

我打算趁寒假的时候去旅行。

Wǒ dǎsuàn chèn hánjià de shíhòu qù lǚxíng。

Practice

Q：你打算什麼時候去遊樂場玩？

你打算什么时候去游乐场玩？

Nǐ dǎsuàn shénme shíhòu qù yóulèchǎng wán？

→A：_____

II. EXERCISE

1. Complete the following dialogues

A：你們排了很久嗎？

你们排了很久吗？

Nǐmen pái le hěn jiǔ ma？

B：是啊，_____，才買到電影票。

是啊，_____，才买到电影票。

Shì a，_____，cái mǎidào diànyǐngpiào。

A：你走了很久嗎？

你走了很久吗？

Nǐ zǒu le hěn jiǔ ma？

B：不，我走了五分鐘，就_____。

不，我走了五分钟，就_____。

Bù，wǒ zǒu le wǔ fēnzhōng，jiù_____。

A：你爲什麼去上海？

你为什么去上海？

Nǐ wèishénme qù Shànghǎi？

B：_____。

A：你打算什麼時候去臺灣？

你打算什么时候去台湾？

Nǐ dǎsuàn shénme shíhòu qù Táiwān？

B：_____ 。

2. Complete the following task

Make a plan for a trip to the theme park.

III. SUPPLEMENTARY EXPLANATION

主題樂園相關生詞：

About Theme Park	環球影城 环球影城	迪士尼樂園 迪斯尼乐园	海洋世界 海洋世界	六旗魔法山 六旗魔法山
Pinyin	Huánqiú yǐng chéng	Dísì ní lèyuán	Hǎiyáng shìjiè	Liù qí mófǎ shān
English	Universal Studio	Disneyland	SeaWorld	Six Flags Magic Mountain

About Theme Park	自由落體 自由落体	摩天輪 摩天轮	旋轉木馬 旋转木马	海盜船 海盗船	咖啡杯 咖啡杯
Pinyin	Zìyóu luò tǐ	Mó tiān lún	Xuánzhuǎnmùmǎ	Hǎi dào chuán	Kāfēi bēi
English	Drop ride	Ferris Wheel	Carousel	Pirate Boat	Spinning Tea Cups

IV. CULTURAL NOTES

Weekend Culture （休閒文化大不同）

The eastern and western take on weekends differs quite a bit. Many westerners love outdoor activities, and during summer they flock to the beach to surf, swim, or suntan on the beach wearing just a bikini. Copper colored skin is seen as a sign of good health. On the other hand, some women in Taiwan avoid the sun at all costs, choosing to carry an umbrella with them wherever they go, even to the beach.

In the west, lots of restaurants and stores close for the weekends, but in Taiwan, Hong Kong, and China, that is when such places get the most business.

The Exam Is Coming Up!

考試快要到了！

Warm Up Activities

1. Do you prefer exams or presentations? Why?
2. Tell us how you prepare for Chinese exams. Do you have any tips to share?

LESSON 1

STORY

The final exam for the Chinese class is coming up next Monday. All students are nervous so they are going to prepare together at the library in these days. Jennifer is going to be other students' tutor.

DIALOGUE

Maria： 期末考試快要到了，我怕念不完。

期末考试快要到了，我怕念不完。

Qímò kǎoshì kuàiyào dào le，wǒ pà niàn bù wán。

Mark： 是啊，這次要考12課，生詞那麼多，怎麼樣才記得住呢？

是啊，这次要考12课，生词那么多，怎么样才记得住呢？

Shì a，zhècì yào kǎo 12 kè，shēngcí nàme duō，zěnmeyàng cái jì de zhù ne？

Jennifer： 只要多複習幾次，就一定記得住！

只要多复习几次，就一定记得住！

Zhǐyào duō fùxí jǐ cì，jiù yídìng jì de zhù！

Mark： 對了！老師說要考是非題、選擇題還有填空，
對嗎？

對了！老师说要考是非题、选择题还有填空，
对吗？

Duìle！Lǎoshī shuō yào kǎo shìfēití、xuǎnzétí háiyǒu
tiánkòng，duìma？

Maria： 嗯，還有簡答題，老師說寫錯一個字扣一分！

嗯，还有简答题，老师说写错一个字扣一分！

En，háiyǒu jiǎndátí，lǎoshī shuō xiěcuò yí ge zì kòu yì
fēn！

DISCUSSION

1. What was Maria worried about?

2. What was Mark's question?

3. What did Jennifer say?

4. What types of questions will be in the exam?

VOCABULARY

	Traditional Character	Simplified Character	Pinyin	English
1	期末	期末	qímò	[名] end of term
2	考試	考试	kǎoshì	[名] test; exam
3	怕	怕	pà	[動] afraid
4	念不完	念不完	niànbùwán	[動] not be able to finish studying/reading a specified portion
5	生詞	生词	shēngcí	[名] new word
6	記得住	记得住	jìdezhù	[動] (be able to) remember
7	複習	复习	fùxí	[動] study; review
8	是非題	是非题	shìfēití	[名] true/false question
9	選擇題	选择题	xuǎnzétí	[名] multiple choice question

	Traditional Character	Simplified Character	Pinyin	English
10	填空	填空	tiánkòng	[名] fill in the blank question
11	簡答題	简答题	jiǎndátí	[名] short answer question
12	寫錯	写错	xiěcuò	[動] write down the wrong answer; write in the wrong way
13	扣分	扣分	kòufēn	[動] to have marks deducted; to lose points

GRAMMAR

1. …快要到了

Examples:

期末考試快要到了。

期末考试快要到了。

Qímò kǎoshì kuàiyào dào le。

中國新年快要到了。

中国新年快要到了。

Zhōngguó xīnnián kuàiyào dào le。

2. V不/得C

Examples:

這麼多功課，我做不完。

这么多功课，我做不完。

Zhème duō gōngkè，wǒ zuò bù wán。

這麼多生詞，我記不住。

这么多生词，我记不住。

Zhème duō shēngcí，wǒ jì bú zhù。

3. 我以爲…

Examples:

我以爲他是日本人。

我以为他是日本人。

Wǒ yǐwéi tā shì Rìběn rén。

我以爲昨天沒有功課。

我以为昨天没有功课。

Wǒ yǐwéi zuótiān méiyǒu gōngkè。

LESSON 2

STORY

The intermediate level class is also having an exam. Ms. Chen is giving the class an oral test. She has every student select a topic related to Chinese culture and also asks them to prepare for a 5-minute presentation.

DIALOGUE

Lin： 你看起來很累？怎麼了？

你看起来很累？怎么了？

Nǐ kànqǐlái hěn lèi？Zěnmele？

Jeff： 我昨天熬夜寫報告，到今天早上四點才睡。

我昨天熬夜寫报告，到今天早上四点才睡。

Wǒ zuótiān áoyè xiě bàogào，dào jīntiān zǎoshang sì diǎn cái shuì。

Lin： 難怪你這麼累。說真的，報告比考試麻煩得多！我寧可考試也不想報告。

难怪你这么累。说真的，报告比考试麻烦得多！我宁可考试也不想报告。

Nánguài nǐ zhème lèi。Shuōzhēnde，bàogào bǐ kǎoshì máfán de duō！Wǒ níngkě kǎoshì yě bùxiǎng bàogào。

Jeff：怎麼可能？報告比較容易吧！只要說話就好，
輕鬆多了。

怎么可能？报告比较容易吧！只要说话就好，
轻松多了。

Zěnmekěnéng？Bàogào bǐjiào róngyì ba！Zhǐyào shuōhuà
jiù hǎo，qīngsōng duō le。

Lin：你別忘了，陳老師特別注意發音，還有，上臺
報告不可以看稿！

你别忘了，陈老师特别注意发音，还有，上台
报告不可以看稿！

Nǐ bié wàng le！Chén lǎoshī tèbié zhùyì fāyīn，háiyǒu，
shàngtái bàogào bùkěyǐ kàn gǎo！

DISCUSSION

1. Why did Jeff look so tired?

2. Does Lin find written test or oral presentation easier? Why?

3. What about Jeff?

VOCABULARY

	Traditional Character	Simplified Character	Pinyin	English
1	熬夜	熬夜	áoyè	[動] burn the midnight oil
2	睡	睡	shuì	[動] sleep
3	麻煩	麻烦	máfán	[形] troublesome
4	輕鬆	轻松	qīngsōng	[形] easy
5	發音	发音	fāyīn	[名] pronunciation
6	上臺	上台	shàngtái	[動] come up to stage
7	看稿	看稿	kàn gǎo	[動] read from notes

EXPRESSION

	Traditional Character	Simplified Character	Pinyin	English
1	說真的	说真的	shuōzhēnde	to be honest
2	怎麼可能	怎么可能	zěnme kěnéng	How is that possible? How is it so?

GRAMMAR

1. 到…才+V

Examples:

我到早上四點才睡。

我到早上四点才睡。

Wǒ dào zǎoshang sì diǎn cái shuì。

我到晚上十點才回家。

我到晚上十点才回家。

Wǒ dào wǎnshang shí diǎn cái huíjiā。

2. 寧可…也不要…

Examples:

我寧可報告，也不要考試。

我宁可报告，也不要考试。

Wǒ níngkě bàogào，yě bùyào kǎoshì。

我寧可不吃，也不要吃他做的菜。

我宁可不吃，也不要吃他做的菜。

Wǒ níngkě bù chī，yě búyào chī tā zuò de cài。

I. PRACTICE

1.

Q：這麼多課，你念得完嗎？

这么多课，你念得完吗？

Zhème duō kè，nǐ niàn de wán ma？

A：

1. 我念不完。

    我念不完。

    Wǒ niàn bù wán。

2. 我念得完。

    我念得完。

    Wǒ niàn de wán。

Practice

Q：這麼多菜，你吃得完嗎？

這么多菜，你吃得完吗？

Zhème duō cài，nǐ chī de wán ma？

→A：＿＿＿＿＿＿＿＿＿

2.

Q：這麼多生詞，怎麼樣才記得住？

這么多生词，怎么样才记得住？

Zhème duō shēngcí，zěnmeyàng cái jì de zhù？

A：只要你多複習幾次，就記得住。

只要你多复习几次，就记得住。

Zhǐyào nǐ duō fùxí jǐ cì，jiù jì de zhù。

Practice

Q：怎麼樣才可以把中文學好？

怎么样才可以把中文学好？

Zěnmeyàng cái kěyǐ bǎ zhōngwén xué hǎo？

→A：＿＿＿＿＿＿＿＿＿

3.

Q：你昨天幾點睡？

你昨天几点睡？

Nǐ zuótiān jǐ diǎn shuì？

A：我熬夜到今天早上四點才睡。

我熬夜到今天早上四点才睡。

Wǒ áoyè dào jīntiān zǎoshang sì diǎn cái shuì。

> **Practice**
>
> Q：你昨天什麼時候回家？
>
> 你昨天什么时候回家？
>
> Nǐ zuótiān shénme shíhòu huíjiā？
>
> →A：＿＿＿＿＿＿＿＿

4.

Q：你不是不喜歡考試嗎？

你不是不喜欢考试吗？

Nǐ búshì bù xǐhuān kǎoshì ma？

A：對，可是我更不喜歡報告，所以我寧可考試，也不要報告。

对，可是我更不喜欢报告，所以我宁可考试，也不要报告。

Duì，kěshì wǒ gèng bù xǐhuān bàogào，suǒyǐ wǒ níngkě kǎoshì，yě búyào bàogào。

> **Practice**
>
> Q：你不是很餓嗎？爲什麼不吃麵包？
>
> 你不是很饿吗？为什么不吃面包？
>
> Nǐ búshì hěn è ma？Wèishénme bù chī miànbāo？
>
> →A：＿＿＿＿＿＿＿＿

II. EXERCISE

1. Complete the following dialogues

A：這些漢字，你都記得住嗎？

這些漢字，你都记得住吗？

Zhèxiē hànzì，nǐ dōu jì de zhù ma？

B：＿＿＿＿＿＿＿＿＿＿。

A：怎麼樣中文才可以說得很好？

怎么样中文才可以说得很好？

Zěnmeyàng Zhōngwén cái kěyǐ shuō de hěn hǎo？

B：只要＿＿＿＿＿，就＿＿＿＿＿。

只要＿＿＿＿＿，就＿＿＿＿＿。

Zhǐyào＿＿＿＿＿，jiù＿＿＿＿＿。

A：你昨天幾點吃晚飯？

你昨天几点吃晚饭？

Nǐ zuótiān jǐ diǎn chī wǎnfàn？

B：＿＿＿＿＿＿＿＿＿＿。

A：你爲什麼不跟他們去看電影？

你为什么不跟他们去看电影？

Nǐ wèishénme bù gēn tāmen qù kàn diànyǐng？

B：我明天要考試，＿＿＿＿＿。

我明天要考试，＿＿＿＿＿。

Wǒ míngtiān yào kǎoshì，＿＿＿＿＿。

2. Complete the following task

A. Have the students share with one another their tips in learning Chinese and remembering new words.

B. Have the students discuss if there should be exams for Chinese classes. What is good about taking exams and what is good about presentations?

III. SUPPLEMENTARY EXPLANATION

考試

exami- nation	小考 小考	期中考 期中考	期末考 期末考	口試 口试	筆試 笔试	閱讀測驗 阅读测验	聽力測驗 听力测验
Pinyin	xiǎokǎo	qízhōng kǎo	qímò kǎo	kǒushì	bǐshì	yuèdú cèyàn	tīnglì cèyàn
English	quiz	mid-term exam	final exam	oral test; presenta-tion	written exam	reading com-prehension	listening com-prehension

IV. CULTURAL NOTES

Education System in Taiwan（臺灣的教育制度）

　　Examination is highly valued in Chinese culture and has been the major way to select talents since ancient times. In the Tang dynasty, the imperial examination system was the only way by which an intellectual can become a civil servant. Ethnic Chinese nowadays see examination as part of their culture and, in Taiwan, Hong Kong, China, and even Japan, there are stringent examination and education systems.

　　Take Taiwan for example, the current education structure is 6-3-3-4: six years of elementary school, three years of junior high school, three years of senior high school, and four years of college or university. Two crucial examinations in this structure control the access to the next level.

　　The first one is the Basic Competence Test used as the basis for entering senior high school from junior high school. Basic Competence Test grants junior high school graduates the tickets to general high school, vocational school, comprehensive high school, or junior college. With the "multiple entrance program" and based on the test score, a student may choose from the various ways to be admitted, such as "recommendation and screening"," guaranteed admission"," voluntary access", or "admission by application".

The second important examination is the college entrance examination. The General Scholastic Ability Test is currently used as the standard examination for college entrance. Based on the test score, a student may choose between "recommendation and screening-based admission" and "admission by placement" to apply for college or university.

The Ministry of Education in Taiwan is currently undertaking education reform, hoping that the students can be released from the burden of exam preparation. However, it is still hard for the students to unhook test results and academic performance because of the pressure from the society and the expectations of parents.

第十二章
UNIT 12

Life in High School
高中生活大不同

Warm Up Activities

1. What life in high school is like in Asian countries to your understanding?
2. Do you know what bǔxí is? Do you think high school students need that?

LESSON 1

STORY

Mark is accepted to the exchange student program. He wants to ask Lin's cousin about the life in Taiwan, and what are some of the things he needs to know as a high school student there.

DIALOGUE

Mark：Lin！你表弟什麼時候有空，我想問他臺灣的生活怎麼樣？

Lin！你表弟什么时候有空，我想问他台湾的生活怎么样？

Lin！Nǐ biǎodì shénme shíhòu yǒukòng，wǒ xiǎng wèn tā Táiwān de shēnghuó zěnmeyàng？

Lin：他最近應該沒有空，他正在準備期末考，下課以後還要去補習，晚上十點才回家。

他最近应该没有空，他正在准备期末考，下课以后还要去补习，晚上十点才回家。

Tā zuìjìn yīnggāi méiyǒukòng，tā zhèng zài zhǔnbèi qímòkǎo，xiàkè yǐhòu háiyào qù bǔxí，wǎnshang shí diǎn cái huíjiā。

Mark：什麼？補習？

什么？补习？

Shénme？Bǔxí？

Lin：你不知道嗎？爲了準備大學考試，臺灣的高中
生一天得念12個鐘頭的書，壓力很大。

你不知道吗？为了准备大学考试，台湾的高中
生一天得念12个钟头的书，压力很大。

Nǐ bù zhīdào ma？Wèile zhǔnbèi dàxué kǎoshì，Táiwān
de gāozhōngshēng yì tiān děi niàn 12 ge zhōngtou de shū，
yālì hěn dà。

Mark：太可憐了！幸好我只是交換生，要不然我一定
受不了！

太可怜了！幸好我只是交换生，要不然我一定
受不了！

Tài kělián le！Xìnghǎo wǒ zhǐ shì jiāohuànsheng，
yàobùrán wǒ yídìng shòubùliǎo！

DISCUSSION

1. What are the questions Mark wants to ask Lin about?
2. Does Lin's cousin have the time for Mark? Why?
3. Is it hard to be a high school student in Taiwan?

VOCABULARY

	Traditioal Character	Simplified Characrer	Pinyin	English
1	表弟	表弟	biǎodì	[名] cousin (younger male from the female line)
	生活	生活	shēnghuó	[名] daylife
2	下課	下课	xiàkè	[動] finish class; get out of class
3	補習	补习	bǔxí	[動] take extra lessons at a cram school
4	大學	大学	dàxué	[名] college; university
5	高中生	高中生	gāozhōngshēng	[名] high school student
6	壓力	压力	yālì	[名] pressure
7	可憐	可怜	kělián	[形] poor
8	受不了	受不了	shòubùliǎo	[動] cannot stand something

GRAMMAR

1. 爲了＋目的，人＋得＋V

Examples:

爲了準備大學考試，高中生得很用功。

为了准备大学考试，高中生得很用功。

Wèile zhǔnbèi dàxué kǎoshì，gāozhōngshēng děi hěn yònggōng。

爲了要有好工作，他得學很多語言。

为了要有好工作，他得学很多語言。

Wèile yào yǒu hǎo gōngzuò，tā děi xué hěn duō yǔyán。

2. 幸好…，要不然…

Examples:

幸好我只是交換生，要不然我一定受不了！

幸好我只是交换生，要不然我一定受不了！

Xìnghǎo wǒ zhǐshì jiāohuànshēng，yàobùrán wǒ yídìng shòubùliǎo！

幸好你帶了錢，要不然我就沒錢吃飯了。

幸好你带了钱，要不然我就没钱吃饭了。

Xìnghǎo nǐ dài le qián，yàobùrán wǒ jiù méi qián chī fàn le。

LESSON 2

Linda and Jeff are both going to Beijing as exchange students. They run into each other today and talk about lodging.

DIALOGUE

Linda： 嗨！Jeff！你什麼時候去北京？
　　　　嗨！Jeff！你什么时候去北京？
　　　　Hāi！Jeff！Nǐ shénme shíhòu qù Běijīng？

Jeff： 八月底吧。我會先打工存錢，開學前一個星期再去。
　　　 八月底吧。我会先打工存钱，开学前一个星期再去。
　　　 Bā yuèdǐ ba。Wǒ huì xiān dǎgōng cún qián，kāixué qián yí ge xīngqí zài qù。

Linda： 我也是。對了！住宿的問題你都安排好了嗎？
　　　　我也是。对了！住宿的问题你都安排好了吗？
　　　　Wǒ yě shì。Duìle！Zhùsù de wèntí nǐ dōu ānpái hǎole ma？

Jeff： 我申請了宿舍，交換學生都住在同一棟大樓，
你呢？

我申请了宿舍，交换学生都住在同一栋大楼，
你呢？

Wǒ shēnqǐng le sùshè, jiāohuàn xuéshēng dōu zhù zài tóng
yí dòng dàlóu, nǐ ne？

Linda： 我申請了寄宿家庭，這樣一來，我有更多機會
瞭解中國人的生活。到時候保持聯絡！

我申请了寄宿家庭，这样一来，我有更多机会
了解中国人的生活。到时候保持联络！

Wǒ shēnqǐng le jìsù jiātíng, zhèyàngyìlái, wǒ yǒu gèng
duō jīhuì liǎojiě Zhōngguórén de shēnghuó。 Dàoshíhòu
bǎochí liánluò！

DISCUSSION

1. When do Linda and Jeff plan on going to China?

2. Where are they going to live in Beijing?

VOCABULARY

	Traditional Character	Simplified Character	Pinyin	English
1	打ㄉㄚˇ工ㄍㄨㄥ	打工	dǎgōng	[動] work part-time
2	存ㄘㄨㄣˊ錢ㄑㄧㄢˊ	存钱	cún qián	[動] save money
3	開ㄎㄞ學ㄒㄩㄝˊ	开学	kāixué	[動] (school) starts
4	住ㄓㄨˋ宿ㄙㄨ	住宿	zhùsù	[動] lodge; get accommodation (in dorm)
5	交ㄐㄧㄠ換ㄏㄨㄢˋ	交换	jiāohuàn	[動] exchange
6	學ㄒㄩㄝˊ生ㄕㄥ	学生	xuésheng	[名] student
7	同ㄊㄨㄥˊ	同	tóng	[形] the same
8	宿ㄙㄨˋ舍ㄕㄜˋ	宿舍	sùshè	[動] dorm
9	棟ㄉㄨㄥˋ	栋	dòng	[量] a measure word used to count buildings
10	大ㄉㄚˋ樓ㄌㄡˊ	大楼	dàlóu	[名] building

	Traditional Character	Simplified Character	Pinyin	English
11	寄ㄐㄧˋ宿ㄙㄨˋ家ㄐㄧㄚ庭ㄊㄧㄥˊ	寄宿家庭	jìsù jiātíng	[名] home stay; host family
12	更ㄍㄥˋ	更	gèng	[副] more
13	機ㄐㄧ會ㄏㄨㄟˋ	机会	jīhuì	[名] opportunity
14	了ㄌㄧㄠˇ解ㄐㄧㄝˇ	了解	liǎojiě	[動] understand
15	到ㄉㄠˋ時ㄕˊ候ㄏㄡˋ	到时候	dàoshíhòu	[副] then (a point of time in the future)

EXPRESSION

	Traditional Character	Simplified Character	Pinyin	English
1	月ㄩㄝˋ底ㄉㄧˇ	月底	yuèdǐ	end of a month
2	保ㄅㄠˇ持ㄔˊ聯ㄌㄧㄢˊ絡ㄌㄨㄛˋ	保持联络	bǎochí liánluò	keep in touch
3	這ㄓㄜˋ樣ㄧㄤˋ一ㄧ來ㄌㄞˊ	这样一来	zhèyàngyìlái	That way, ...

GRAMMAR

1. 同一+量+N

Examples:

同一棟大樓

同一栋大楼

Tóng yí dòng dàlóu

同一個教室

同一个教室

Tóng yí ge jiàoshì

2. 這樣一來

Examples:

我跟中國人一起生活，這樣一來，就更瞭解他們的文化。

我跟中国人一起生活，这样一来，就更了解他们的文化。

Wǒ gēn Zhōngguórén yìqǐ shēnghuó, zhèyàngyìlái, jiù gèng liǎojiě tāmen de wénhuà。

上課要注意，這樣一來，才能聽懂老師說的。

上课要注意，这样一来，才能听懂老师说的。

Shàngkè yào zhùyì, zhèyàngyìlái, cái néng tīngdǒng lǎoshī shuō de。

I. PRACTICE

1.

Q：他爲什麼看起來這麼累？

他为什么看起来这么累？

Tā wèishénme kànqǐlái zhème lèi？

A：因爲他爲了存錢出國，每天工作12個鐘頭。

因为他为了存钱出国，每天工作12个钟头。

Yīnwèi tā wèile cún qián chūguó, měitiān gōngzuò 12 ge zhōngtou。

> **Practice**
>
> Q：爲什麼小王這幾天都去電影院？
>
> 为什么小王这几天都去电影院？
>
> Wèishénme Xiǎo Wáng zhè jǐ tiān dōu qù diànyǐngyuàn？
>
> →A：_____

2.

Q：我忘了帶錢，怎麼辦？

我忘了带钱，怎么办？

Wǒ wàng le dàiqián，zěnmebàn？

A：幸好我帶了，要不然你就不能吃飯了！

幸好我带了，要不然你就不能吃饭了！

Xìnghǎo wǒ dài le，yàobùrán nǐ jiù bùnéng chī fàn le！

Practice

Q：下雨了，怎麼辦？

下雨了，怎么办？

Xià yǔ le，zěnmebàn？

→A：_____

3.

Q：住宿的問題，你都安排好了嗎？

住宿的问题，你都安排好了吗？

Zhùsù de wèntí，nǐ dōu ānpái hǎole ma？

A：

1. 都安排好了。

都安排好了。

Dōu ānpái hǎole。

2. 還沒，我還沒找到住的地方。

还没，我还没找到住的地方。

Háiméi，wǒ háiméi zhǎodào zhù de dìfāng。

Practice

Q：出國的事，你都安排好了嗎？

出国的事，你都安排好了吗？

Chūguó de shì , nǐ dōu ānpái hǎole ma ？

→A：_____

II. EXERCISE

1. Complete the following dialogues

A：爲什麼你想學中文呢？

为什么你想学中文呢？

Wèishénme nǐ xiǎng xué Zhōngwén ne ？

B：我是爲了_____。

我是为了_____。

Wǒ shì wèile_____。

A：我忘了準備報告了，怎麼辦？

我忘了准备报告了，怎么办？

Wǒ wàng le zhǔnbèi bàogào le , zěnmebàn ？

B：幸好_____，要不然_____。

幸好_____，要不然_____。

Xìnghǎo_____， yàobùrán_____。

A：交換計畫，你都申請好了嗎？

交换计划，你都申请好了吗？

Jiāohuàn jìhuà , nǐ dōu shēnqǐng hǎole ma ？

B：_____。

2. Complete the following task

A. Have the students list 10 things that they think they must do if they are an exchange student in either China or Taiwan. Have them explain the reasons why.

B. If there are exchange students from an Asian country in the class, have other students interview them on the high school life in the country they are from.

III. SUPPLEMENTARY EXPLANATION

各地教育制度的差別

	臺灣 Taiwan	美國 United States	中國大陸 China
學制 Structure	小學6年+國中3年+ 高中3年+大學4年 6 years of elementary school + 3 years of junior high school + 3 years of senior high school + 4 years of college or university	小學5年+國中3年+ 高中4年+大學4年 5 years of elementary school + 3 years of junior high school + 4 years of senior high school + 4 years of college or university	小學6年+國中3年+ 高中3年+大學4年 6 years of elementary school + 3 years of junior high school + 3 years of senior high school + 4 years of college or university

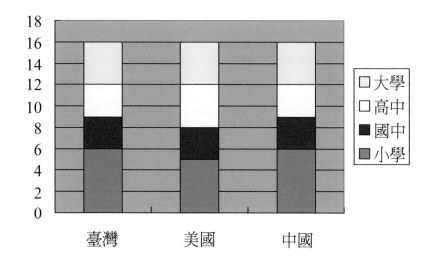

IV. CULTURAL NOTES

Introducing Beijing（北京簡介）

Beijing is the political, economic, and cultural center of China and also an ancient city with a history of 3 millennia. Along the course of the history, five dynasties chose this city as their capital. Beijing is thus characterized by an abundance of cultural and historical sites and many of them are listed among the UNESCO world heritage sites, such as the largest palace in the world – the Forbidden City, royal park – the Summer Palace, the Temple of Heaven where emperors worshipped the god of heaven, the Ming tombs where the Chinese Ming Dynasty emperors were buried, the world famous Badaling section of the Great Wall, and etc. A tour in Beijing would equal to a tour of the many thousand years of the history of China.

The de facto population of Beijing has exceeded 20 million. The urban area has also been expanding in size. The best way to travel Beijing city is by subway. The subway routes cover most tourist attractions and also reach Beijing Capital International Airport and other airports in the city. It goes to every corner of the city with a rather low ticket price.

Beijing has been developed into an international metropolitan, yet when you explore the "hutongs" (alleyways), you get to experience the lifestyle of old "Beijingers". The city where history and modernity meet is now facing a new challenge: the dust storms from north and serious air pollution are clouding the city's blue sky. This is something that needs to be solved as soon as possible.

Vocabulary Index

	Vocabulary	Simplified Character	Pinyin	Explanation	Unit
1	安排	安排	ānpái	arrange	10
2	熬夜	熬夜	áoyè	burn the midnight oil	11
3	把	把	bǎ	a particle making the following noun as a direct object	7
4	半	半	bàn	helf	10
5	半個小時	半个小时	bàn ge xiǎoshí	half an hour	5
6	磅	磅	bàng	pound	8
7	包	包	bāo	wrap	7
8	抱怨	抱怨	bàoyuàn	complain	10
9	杯	杯	bēi	measure word：glass	6
10	本來	本来	běnlái	originally	8
11	比	比	bǐ	a preposition used to make comparison	2
12	表弟	表弟	biǎodì	cousin (younger male from the female line)	12
13	表演	表演	biǎoyǎn	performance	4
14	別	别	bié	do not	10
15	別的	别的	biéde	other things	10
16	比賽	比赛	bǐsài	game (n.) play (v.)	8
17	鼻子	鼻子	bízi	nose	4
18	部	部	bù	measure word used to count movies	5

	Vocabulary	Simplified Character	Pinyin	Explanation	Unit
19	不必	不必	búbì	not having to	4
20	不同	不同	bùtóng	different	1
21	補習	补习	bǔxí	take extra lessons at a cram school	12
22	才	才	cái	only	7
23	才	才	cái	not…until	10
24	材料	材料	cáiliào	ingredient	7
25	茶	茶	chá	tea	1
26	場	场	chǎng	a measure word used to count the number of sporting activities	8
27	嘗嘗	尝尝	cháng cháng	taste	2
28	唱歌	唱歌	chàng gē	sing	4
29	趁	趁	chèn	when; during	10
30	成績單	成绩单	chéngjīdān	transcript	9
31	城市	城市	chéngshì	city	1
32	遲到	到	chídào	being late	5
33	抽空	抽空	chōukòng	to allocate time for something	3
34	穿	穿	chuān	wear	8
35	初級班／班	初级班／班	chūjí bān/bān	elementary level; elementary class/class	4
36	春天	春天	chūntiān	spring	3
37	次	次	cì	a measure word used to count numerated events (time)	8

	Vocabulary	Simplified Character	Pinyin	Explanation	Unit
38	刺激	刺激	cìjī	excite	10
39	存錢	存	cún qián	save money	12
40	打工	打工	dǎgōng	work part-time	12
41	帶	帶	dài	take (a person somewhere)	1
42	帶來	带来	dàilái	bring	2
43	大樓	大楼	dàlóu	building	12
44	當然	当然	dāngrán	of course; sure	5
45	到時候	到时候	dàoshíhòu	then (a point of time in the future)	12
46	打拳	打拳	dǎquán	fight; do a specific kind of martial art	4
47	大學	大学	dàxué	college; university	12
48	得到	得到	dédào	obtain; get	8
49	得	得	děi	have to	6
50	等	等	děng	wait	5
51	點心	点心	diǎnxīn	light refreshment	2
52	電影院	电影院	diàn yǐng yuàn	movie theater	5
53	地方	地方	dìfāng	place	1
54	棟	栋	dòng	a measure word used to count buildings	12
55	動物	动物	dòngwù	animal	2
56	動作	动作	dòngzuò	move	8
57	短劇	短剧	duǎn jù	skit	4

	Vocabulary	Simplified Character	Pinyin	Explanation	Unit
58	多	多	duō	more	7
59	讀書計畫	读书计划	dúshū jìhuà	statement of purpose; study plan	9
60	嗯	嗯	en	oh	8
61	發白	发白	fābái	turn pal; turn white	10
62	放	放	fàng	put	7
63	方形	方形	fāng xíng	square	2
64	放鬆	放松	fàngsōng	relax	10
65	反正	反正	fǎnzhèng	anyway	10
66	發音	发音	fāyīn	pronunciation	11
67	分	分	fēn	point; score	8
68	分鐘	分钟	fēnzhōng	minute	10
69	複習	复习	fùxí	study; review	11
70	…感	…感	gǎn	sense (of)	10
71	剛剛	刚刚	gānggāng	just then	10
72	趕快	赶快	gǎnkuài	hurry	10
73	高	高	gāo	high	4
74	高中生	高中生	gāo zhōng shēng	high school student	12
75	跟	跟	gēn	with	4
76	根	根	gēn	a measure word used to count items that shape like sticks	7
77	更	更	gèng	more	12
78	更	更	gèng	even more	1

	Vocabulary	Simplified Character	Pinyin	Explanation	Unit
79	功夫片	功夫片	gōngfu piàn	action movie	5
80	逛	逛	guàng	stroll	1
81	逛街	逛街	guàngjiē	shop	6
82	關係	关系	guānxì	related to; having to do with	5
83	關於	关于	guānyú	about	9
84	過來	过来	guò lái	come here	1
85	古色古香	古色古香	Gǔ sè gǔ xiāng	traditional	1
86	嗨	嗨	hài	hi	9
87	還有	还有	hái yǒu	also	2
88	還好	还好	háihǎo	luckily	4
89	寒假/暑假	寒假/暑假	hánjià/shǔjià	winter vacation/summer vacation	1
90	好	好	hǎo	ready	7
91	好好地	好好地	hǎohǎode	well; properly	10
92	喝	喝	hē	drink	1
93	紅	红	hóng	red	3
94	後來	后来	hòulái	afterwards	8
95	會	会	huì	can (to be able to)	8
96	活動	活动	huódòng	event; activity	3
97	擠	挤	jǐ	crowded	5
98	加緊	加紧	jiājǐn	hurry to do something; more often to do something	8

	Vocabulary	Simplified Character	Pinyin	Explanation	Unit
99	煎	煎	jiān	pan-fry	7
100	簡答題	简答题	jiǎndátí	short answer question	11
101	獎學金	奖学金	jiǎngxuéjīn	scholarship	9
102	健康	健康	jiànkāng	healthy	7
103	建築	建筑	jiànzhú	building; architecture	1
104	交換	交换	jiāohuàn	exchange	12
105	交換計畫	交换计划	jiāohuàn jìhuà	exchange program	9
106	郊外	郊外	jiāowài	suburb	10
107	假期	假期	jiàqí	vacation	10
108	記得住	得住	jìdezhù	(be able to) remember	11
109	節目	节目	jiémù	events	4
110	節目單	节目单	jiémù dān	list of events	4
111	結束	结束	jiéshù	end	10
112	機會	机会	jīhuì	opportunity	12
113	季節	季节	jìjié	season	10
114	緊張	紧张	jǐnzhāng	nervous	8
115	寄宿家庭	寄宿家庭	jìsù jiātíng	home stay; host family	12
116	捲 捲起來	卷 卷起来	juǎn juǎnqǐ lái	roll	7
117	咖啡	咖啡	kāfēi	coffee	6
118	開學	开学	kāixué	(school) starts	12

	Vocabulary	Simplified Character	Pinyin	Explanation	Unit
119	看稿	看稿	kàn gǎo	read from notes	11
120	考試	考试	kǎoshì	test; exam	11
121	可憐	可怜	kělián	poor	12
122	扣分	扣分	kòufēn	to have marks deducted; to lose points	11
123	快	快	kuài	hurry	1
124	來	来	lái	come	7
125	籃球	篮球	lánqiú	basketball	6
126	累	累	lèi	tired; tiring	8
127	臉色	脸色	liǎnsè	complexion	10
128	練習	练习	liànxí	practice	4
129	聊	聊	liáo	chat; talk	7
130	瞭解	了解	liǎojiě	understand	12
131	聊天	聊天	liáotiān	chat	3
132	留學	留学	liúxué	study overseas; study abroad	9
133	禮物	礼物	lǐwù	gift	2
134	輪到	轮到	lúndào	being someone's turn	4
135	麻煩	麻烦	máfán	troublesome	11
136	慢	慢	màn	slow	5
137	忙	忙	máng	busy	8
138	忙著	忙着	mángzhe	busy doing something	6
139	沒空	没空	méikòng	busy; having had plans	6

	Vocabulary	Simplified Character	Pinyin	Explanation	Unit
140	美味	美味	měiwèi	delicious; tasty	1
141	門	门	mén	door	3
142	名產	名产	míngchǎn	specialty goods	2
143	祕書	祕书	mìshū	secretary	9
144	拿	拿	ná	take	3
145	難怪	难怪	nánguài	no wonder	4
146	難看	难看	nánkàn	ugly	7
147	念不完	念不完	niànbùwán	not be able to finish studying/ reading a specified portion	11
148	喔	喔	ō	phew	4
149	怕	怕	pà	afraid	11
150	拍	拍	pāi	take (photo)	1
151	排隊	排队	páiduì	line up; queue	10
152	拍照	拍照	pāizhào	take pictures	6
153	胖	胖	pàng	overweight	8
154	陪	陪	péi	accompany	6
155	碰面	碰面	pèngmiàn	meet	5
156	期末	期末	qímò	end of term	11
157	清楚	清楚	qīngchǔ	clear	9
158	輕鬆	轻松	qīngsōng	easy	11
159	慶祝	庆祝	qìngzhù	celebrate	3
160	全家	全家	quán jiā	the whole family	3

	Vocabulary	Simplified Character	Pinyin	Explanation	Unit
161	讓	让	ràng	to cause	1
162	熱鬧	热闹	rènào	crowded; busy	1
163	容易	容易	róngyì	easy	7
164	上山	上山	shàng shān	go to the mountains	1
165	上面	上面	shàngmiàn	on	2
166	上臺	上台	shàngtái	come up to stage	11
167	生詞	生词	shēngcí	new word	11
168	生活	生活	shēnghuó	daylife	12
169	申請	申请	shēnqǐng	apply	9
170	試	试	shì	try	6
171	是非題	是非题	shìfēití	true/false question	11
172	食物	食物	shíwù	food	9
173	適應	适应	shìyìng	adapt to; fit in	9
174	熟	熟	shóu	cooked	7
175	瘦	瘦	shòu	slim; skinny	8
176	首	首	shǒu	a measure word used to count songs	4
177	售票口 門口 電影票	售票口 门口 电影票	shòu piào kǒu ménkǒu diànyǐng piào	ticketing booth gate; door movie ticket	5
178	屬	属	shǔ	belong to	2
179	輸	输	shū	lose	8

	Vocabulary	Simplified Character	Pinyin	Explanation	Unit
180	睡	睡	shuì	sleep	11
181	睡覺	睡觉	shuìjiào	sleep	3
182	算	算	suàn	calculate	9
183	雖然	虽然	suīrán	although	8
184	宿舍	宿舍	sùshè	dorm	12
185	特別	特别	tèbié	special	2
186	特產	特产	tèchǎn	local cuisine; specialty	2
187	踢	踢	tī	kick	4
188	甜	甜	tián	sweet	2
189	填空	填空	tiánkòng	fill in the blank question	11
190	天氣	天气	tiānqì	weather	9
191	天天	天天	tiāntiān	everyday	8
192	跳	跳	tiào	jump; leap	8
193	貼	贴	tiē	stick	3
194	同	同	tóng	the same	12
195	同學	同学	tóngxué	student; classmate	3
196	投進	投进	tóujìn	shoot in	8
197	吐	吐	tù	vomit; throw up	10
198	推薦信	推荐信	tuījiànxìn	recommendation letter	9
199	外婆	外婆	wàipó	grandmother	7
200	完	完	wán	finish	3

	Vocabulary	Simplified Character	Pinyin	Explanation	Unit
201	晚飯	晚饭	wǎn fàn	dinner	3
202	網路	网络	wǎnglù	internet	1
203	晚會	晚会	wǎnhuì	party; event (usually held in the evening)	4
204	晚上	晚上	wǎnshang	evening; night	1
205	味道	味道	wèidào	taste	2
206	爲了	了	wèile	for	10
207	問	问	wèn	ask	6
208	文化	文化	wénhuà	culture	9
209	問題	问题	wèntí	question	6
210	嚇	吓	xià	scare; frighten	10
211	下車	下车	xià chē	get off	5
212	下課	下课	xiàkè	finish class; get out of class	12
213	香	香	xiāng	having a pleasant smell	7
214	想念	想念	xiǎngniàn	miss	10
215	現在	现在	xiànzài	now	3
216	小 / 大	小 / 大	xiǎo/ dà	young; small; little/ old;big;large	2
217	小吃	小吃	xiǎochī	snack	1
218	小時	小时	xiǎoshí	hour	4
219	寫	写	xiě	write	3
220	寫錯	写错	xiěcuò	write down the wrong answer; write in the wrong way	11

	Vocabulary	Simplified Character	Pinyin	Explanation	Unit
221	行程	行程	xíngchéng	plan; schedule	10
222	選課	选课	xuǎn kè	enroll (in class)	9
223	選擇題	选择题	xuǎnzétí	multiple choice question	11
224	學分	学分	xuéfēn	credit	9
225	學生	学生	xuésheng	student	12
226	學校	学校	xuéxiào	school	9
227	壓力	压力	yālì	pressure	12
228	要求	要求	yāoqiú	requirement	9
229	鑰匙 / 鑰匙圈	钥匙 / 钥匙圈	yàoshi/ yàoshi quān	key/ key chain	2
230	一秒鐘	一秒钟	yì miǎozhōng	one second	8
231	一定	一定	yídìng	certainly	5
232	衣服	衣服	yīfú	clothing; top	8
233	已經	已经	yǐjīng	already	7
234	贏	赢	yíng	win	8
235	以前	以前	yǐqián	a point of time before	2
236	藝術	艺术	yìshù	art	6
237	意思	意思	yìsi	meaning	3
238	以為	以为	yǐwéi	thought	7
239	一些	一些	yìxiē	some	9
240	一陣子	一阵子	yízhènzi	a while	10

	Vocabulary	Simplified Character	Pinyin	Explanation	Unit
241	用	用	yòng	similar to the expression of "with"	2
242	有興趣	有兴趣	yǒu xìngqù	interested	5
243	尤其是	尤其是	yóuqí shì	especially	1
244	有趣	有趣	yǒuqù	interesting	3
245	有事	有事	yǒushì	something come up	9
246	圓形 / 圓	圆形 / 圆	yuán xíng/ yuán	circle	2
247	遇到	遇到	yùdào	meet; run into	6
248	約	约	yuē	invite	5
249	運動	运动	yùndòng	exercise	8
250	早上	早上	zǎoshang	morning	1
251	炸	炸	zhà	fry	7
252	展覽	展览	zhǎnlǎn	exhibition	6
253	找	找	zhǎo	find	9
254	這些	这些	zhè xiē	these	1
255	這麼	这么	zhème	this much; to a certain degree	7
256	整個	整个	zhěng ge	whole; entire	3
257	正在	正在	zhèngzài	an adverb used to express an ongoing action	8
258	紙	纸	zhǐ	paper	3
259	只	只	zhǐ	only	6
260	枝	枝	zhī	a measure word used to count pens	3

	Vocabulary	Simplified Character	Pinyin	Explanation	Unit
261	只要	只要	zhǐyào	just	7
262	只有	只有	zhǐyǒu	only	7
263	中部	中部	zhōng bù	the middle part of an area	2
264	中飯 / 晚飯 / 早飯	中饭 / 晚饭 / 早饭	zhōngfàn/ wǎnfàn/ zǎofàn	lunch/ dinner/ breakfast	10
265	鐘頭	钟头	zhōngtou	hour	10
266	重要	重要	zhòngyào	important	9
267	煮	煮	zhǔ	cook	7
268	主持人	主持人	zhǔchí rén	host; master of ceremony	4
269	準備	准备	zhǔnbèi	prepare	3
270	住宿	住宿	zhùsù	lodge; get accommodation (in dorm)	12
271	注意	注意	zhùyì	be careful	9
272	字	字	zì	word; character	3
273	自傳	自传	zìzhuàn	autobiography; personal statement	9
274	最	最	zuì	most	1
275	最後	最后	zuìhòu	at last	4
276	最近	最近	zuìjìn	recently	5
277	最少	最少	zuìshǎo	at least	4
278	做報告 / 報告	做报告 / 报告	zuò bàogào/ bàogào	write a paper/ report	6

Terms Index

	Vocabulary	Simplified Character	Pinyin	Explanation	Unit
1	表弟	表弟	biǎodì	cousin (male, younger, either from your mother's family or your father's sister's family)	1
2	博物館	博物馆	bówùguǎn	museum	1
3	春捲	春卷	chūnjuǎn	spring roll	7
4	春聯	春联	chūnlián	spring festival couplet	3
5	鳳梨	凤梨	fènglí	Pineapple	2
6	鳳梨酥	凤梨酥	Fènglísū	pineapple cake	2
7	復活節	复活节	Fùhuójié	Easter	10
8	恭喜	恭喜	Gōngxǐ	an expression used to wish others a good luck; similar to congratulations	3
9	冠軍	冠军	guànjūn	champion; championship	8
10	餃子	饺子	jiǎozi	dumpling	7
11	老虎 /虎	老虎 /虎	lǎohǔ/hǔ	tiger	2
12	毛筆	毛笔	máobǐ	brush	3
13	泡溫泉	泡温泉	pào wēnquán	hot spring bathing	1
14	三分球	三分球	sānfēnqiú	three pointer	8
15	聖誕節	圣诞节	Shèngdànjié	Christmas	3
16	生肖	生肖	shēngxiào	Chinese Zodiac	2
17	書法	书法	shūfǎ	calligraphy	3
18	太陽餅	太阳饼	Tài yáng bǐng	Suncake	2

	Vocabulary	Simplified Character	Pinyin	Explanation	Unit
19	兔子 / 兔	兔子 / 兔	tùzi/tù	rabbit	2
20	武術	武术	wǔshù	martial arts	4
21	餡兒	馅儿	xiànér	stuffing	7
22	小籠包	小笼包	Xiǎo lóng bāo	Xiaolongbao	1
23	夜市	夜市	yèshì	night market	1
24	遊樂場	游乐场	yóulèchǎng	theme park	10
25	月餅	月饼	yuèbǐng	Moon cake	2
26	雲霄飛車	云霄飞车	Yún xiāo fēi chē	rollercoaster	10
27	豫園	豫园	Yùyuán	Yu Garden	1
28	中國新年	中国新年	Zhōngguó xīn nián	Chinese New Year; Lunar New Year	3

Expressions Index

	Vocabulary	Simplified Character	Pinyin	Explanation	Unit
1	唉	唉	āi	Oh	5
2	唉呀	唉呀	āiya	Oops	4
3	保持聯絡	保持联络	bǎochí lián-luò	keep in touch	12
4	別管我	别管我	bié guǎn wǒ	leave me alone	10
5	差一點就	差一点就	chāyìdiǎn jiù	an expression used to mean when something almost happened	8
6	吃得到	吃得到	chīdédào	an expression used to mean when some food is available	7
7	穿不下	穿不下	chuān búxià	(clothing) does not fit (because the size is too small)	8
8	春暖花開	春暖花开	Chūn nuǎn huā kāi	flowers blossom as it turns warm in the spring	10
9	當然有	当然有	dāngrán yǒu	Of course	5
10	等一下	等一下	děngyíxià	later	7
11	第二天	第二天	dì èr tiān	second day	3
12	放鬆一下	放松一下	fàngsōng yíxià	relax for a while	10
13	跟…一樣	跟…一样	gēn… yíyàng	like; as	3
14	好幾個	好几个	hǎo jǐ ge	many	8
15	好了	好了	hǎo le	okay; enough of something	7
16	好主意	好主意	hǎo zhǔyì	good idea	10
17	好久不見	好久不见	hǎojiǔbújiàn	It's been so long	1
18	加油	加油	jiāyóu	Go (used as pep talk)	8

	Vocabulary	Simplified Character	Pinyin	Explanation	Unit
19	就這麼說定了	就这么说定了	jiù zhème shuōdìng le	Done deal	10
20	就是啊	就是啊	jiùshì a	I know Exactly	10
21	就行了	就行了	jiùxíngle	an expression used to mean that something would be ready or done after some preceding action	7
22	就要…了	就要…了	jiùyào…le	an expression used to mean when something is about to happen	8
23	可是	可是	kěshì	but	3
24	來不及	来不及	láibùjí		5
25	沒想到	没想到	méi xiǎng dào	did not expect	7
26	你還好嗎？	你还好吗?	nǐ hái hǎo ma	Are you okay?	10
27	念念不忘	念念不忘	Niànniàn-búwàng	unforgettable	1
28	前一天	前一天	qián yì tiān	the day before	3
29	前一陣子	前一阵子	qián yízhènzi	a while ago	10
30	入境隨俗	入境随俗	Rùjìngsuísú	do as the natives do	9
31	少來了	少来了	shǎoláile	C'mon	5
32	…什麼的	…什么的	shénmede	…and such	6
33	說真的	说真的	shuōzhēnde	to be honest	11
34	算了吧	算了吧	suànleba	Forget about it	6
35	天天	天天	tiāntiān	everyday	1
36	我也是	我也是	wǒ yěshì	same with me; I am with you	8

	Vocabulary	Simplified Character	Pinyin	Explanation	Unit
37	我怎麼沒想到？	我怎么没想到?	wǒ zěnme méi xiǎngdào	How could I not think of that?	5
38	想辦法	想办法	xiǎng bànfǎ	try to ; attempt to	9
39	嚇死我了	吓死我了	xiàsǐ wǒ le	I am scared to death	10
40	學不會	学不会	xué búhuì	not able to understand after learning; not able to master something after practicing	8
41	咦	咦	yí	similar to the expression of hmm; huh	2
42	一塊兒	一块儿	yíkuàir	together	1
43	因爲	因为	yīnwèi	because	2
44	月底	月底	yuèdǐ	end of a month	12
45	糟糕	糟糕	zāogāo	Oh No	4
46	怎麼可能	怎么可能	zěnme kěnéng	How is that possible? How is it so?	11
47	怎麼樣	怎么样	zěnmeyàng	How is it?	1
48	這幾天	这几天	zhè jǐ tiān	recently; these days	8
49	眞巧	真巧	zhēn qiǎo	What a coincidence	6
50	這樣一來	这样一来	zhèyàngyìlái	That way, ...	12
51	祝你好運	祝你好运	zhù nǐ hǎoyùn	Good luck	9

Supplement Explanation Index

	Vocabulary	Simplified Character	Pinyin	Explanation	Unit
1	棒球	棒球	bàngqiú	baseball	8
2	北京烤鴨	北京烤鸭	Běijīng kǎoyā	Peking duck	7
3	筆	笔	bǐ	ink brush	3
4	病假	病假	bìngjià	sick leave	1
5	筆試	笔试	bǐshì	written exam	11
6	必修	必修	bìxiū	required course; compulsory course	9
7	炒	炒	chǎo	sauté; stir-fry	7
8	炒米粉	炒米粉	Chǎo mǐfěn	Fried rice noodles	1
9	臭豆腐	臭豆腐	Chòu dòufu	Stinky Tofu	1
10	春	春	chūn	spring	3
11	春假	春假	chūn jià	Chinese spring break	1
12	春節	春节	Chūn Jié	Chinese New Year/Spring Festival	1
13	打太極拳	打太极拳	dǎ tàijíquán	Tai Chi	8
14	大吉大利	大吉大利	Dàjídàlì	great auspice; good luck to you	3
15	淡	淡	dàn	mild; light	7
16	登山	登山	dēngshān	Mountain climbing	8
17	雕塑展	雕塑展	diāosù zhǎn	Sculpture Exhibition	6
18	迪士尼樂園	迪士尼乐园	Dísì ní lèyuán	Disneyland	10
19	豆漿	豆浆	Dòujiāng	Soybean Milk	1

	Vocabulary	Simplified Character	Pinyin	Explanation	Unit
20	端午節	端午节	Duānwǔjié	Dragon Boat Festival	1
21	鳳梨酥	凤梨酥	Fènglí sū	Pineapple cake	1
22	福	福	fú	good fortune; luck; happiness	3
23	感恩節	感恩节	Gǎnēnjié	Thanksgiving	1
24	橄欖球	橄榄球	gǎnlǎnqiú	football	8
25	宮保雞丁	宫保鸡丁	Gōngbǎojīdīng	Kung pao chicken	7
26	恭喜發財	恭喜发财	Gōngxǐfācái	may you be prosperous; may you have a prosperous New Year	3
27	狗	狗	gǒu	Dog	2
28	海盜船	海盗船	Hǎi dào chuán	pirate boat	10
29	海洋世界	海洋世界	Hǎiyáng shìjiè	SeaWorld	10
30	寒假	寒假	hánjià	winter break	1
31	紅燒	红烧	hóngshāo	braise in brown sauce	7
32	紅燒牛肉麵	红烧牛肉面	Hóng shāo niú ròu miàn	Braised beef noodle soup	7
33	猴	猴	hóu	Monkey	2
34	虎	虎	hǔ	Tiger	2
35	環球影城	环球影城	Huánqiú yǐng chéng	Universal Studio	10
36	滑雪	滑雪	huáxuě	skiing	8
37	畫展	画展	huàzhǎn	Art Exhibition	6
38	雞	鸡	jī	Rooster	2

	Vocabulary	Simplified Character	Pinyin	Explanation	Unit
39	煎	煎	jiān	pan-fry	7
40	健行	健行	jiàn xíng	hiking; power walk	8
41	繳費	缴费	jiǎofèi	pay	9
42	咖啡杯	咖啡杯	Kāfēi bēi	Spinning Tea Cups	10
43	烤	烤	kǎo	grill	7
44	口試	口试	kǒushì	oral test; presentation	11
45	苦	苦	kǔ	bitter	7
46	辣	辣	là	hot; spicy	7
47	六旗魔法山	六旗魔法山	Liù qí mófǎ shān	Six Flags Magic Mountain	10
48	龍	龙	lóng	Dragon	2
49	滷	卤	lǔ	stew	7
50	麻	麻	má	numbing	7
51	馬	马	mǎ	Horse	2
52	慢跑	慢跑	mànpǎo	jogging	8
53	麻婆豆腐	麻婆豆腐	Mápódòufu	Hot and spicy tofu	7
54	墨	墨	mò	Chinese ink; ink stick	3
55	摩天輪	摩天轮	Mó tiān lún	Ferris Wheel	10
56	年假	年假	nián jiǎ	Chinese New Year break	1
57	牛	牛	niú	Ox	2
58	牛肉麵	牛肉面	Niúròumiàn	Beef Noodle Soup	1
59	濃	浓	nóng	thick; rich	7

	Vocabulary	Simplified Character	Pinyin	Explanation	Unit
60	排球	排球	páiqiú	volleyball	8
61	乒乓球	乒乓球	pīngpāngqiú	ping pong; table tennis	8
62	騎腳踏車	骑脚踏车	qí jiǎtàchē	biking	8
63	氣功	气功	qìgōng	qigong	5
64	期末考	期末考	qímò kǎo	final exam	11
65	輕功	轻功	qīng gōng	qinggong	5
66	清炒蝦仁	清炒虾仁	Qīngchǎoxiārén	Sautéed shrimp	7
67	清明節	清明节	Qīngmíngjié	Tomb Sweeping Day	1
68	期中考	期中考	qízhōng kǎo	mid-term exam	11
69	燒餅油條	烧饼油条	Shāobǐng yóutiáo	Fried dough stick wrapped in a baked roll	1
70	少林派	少林派	shàolínpài	Shaolin Sect	5
71	蛇	蛇	shé	Snake	2
72	設計展	设计展	shèjì zhǎn	design exhibition	6
73	聖誕節	圣诞节	Shèngdàn Jié	Christmas	1
74	攝影展	影展	shèyǐngzhǎn	Photography exhibition	6
75	事假	事假	shì jià	personal leave	1
76	鼠	鼠	shǔ	Rat	2
77	暑假	暑假	shǔjià	summer break	1
78	酸	酸	suān	sour	7
79	太極拳	太极拳	tàijíquán	Tai chi chuan	5
80	甜	甜	tián	sweet	7

	Vocabulary	Simplified Character	Pinyin	Explanation	Unit
81	跳繩	跳绳	tiàoshéng	jumping rope	8
82	聽力測驗	听力测验	tīnglì cèyàn	listening comprehension	11
83	兔	兔	tù	Rabbit	2
84	萬事如意	万事如意	Wàn shì rúyì	wish you all the best	3
85	網球	网球	wǎngqiú	tennis	8
86	文物展	文物展	wén wù zhǎn	Cultural relics exhibition	6
87	武當派	武当派	wǔ dāngpài	Wudang Sect; Wu-tang clan	5
88	鹹	咸	xián	salty	7
89	小考	小考	xiǎokǎo	quiz	11
90	小籠包	小笼包	Xiǎolóngbāo	xiaolongbao/steamed meat buns	1
91	選修	选修	xuǎnxiū	elective course	9
92	旋轉木馬	旋转木马	Xuán zhuǎn mù mǎ	Carousel	10
93	學費	学费	xuéfèi	tuition	9
94	硯	砚	yàn	inkstone	3
95	羊	羊	yáng	Goat	2
96	影展	影展	yǐngzhǎn	movie festival	6
97	詠春拳	咏春拳	yǒngchūnquán	Wing Chun	5
98	游泳	游泳	yóuyǒng	swimming	8
99	元宵節	元宵节	Yuánxiāojié	Lantern Festival	1
100	閱讀測驗	阅读测验	yuèdú cèyàn	reading comprehension	11

	Vocabulary	Simplified Character	Pinyin	Explanation	Unit
101	瑜珈	瑜珈	yújiā	yoga	8
102	炸	炸	zhá	fry	7
103	蒸	蒸	zhēng	steam	7
104	珍珠奶茶	珍珠奶茶	Zhēnzhū nǎichá	Bubble Tea/Pearl milk tea/Boba	1
105	紙	纸	zhǐ	paper	3
106	中元節	中元	Zhōng yuán jié	Hungry Ghost Festival	1
107	中秋節	中秋	Zhōngqiūjié	Mid-Autumn Festival	1
108	煮	煮	zhǔ	cook; boil	7
109	豬	猪	zhū	Pig	2
110	註冊	注册	zhùcè	register	9
111	住宿	住宿	zhùsù	student housing	9
112	自由落體	自由落体	Zìyóu luò tǐ	Drop ride	10
113	足球	足球	zúqiú	soccer	8

Note

Note

國家圖書館出版品預行編目資料

青春華語（二）/信世昌主編 -- 初版. -- 臺北市：五南，2015.12

　冊；　公分

ISBN 978-957-11-8407-4（第2冊：平裝）

1.漢語 2.讀本

802.86　　　　　　　　　　104024340

1X8G　華語(Chinese)

YOUTH MANDARIN TEXTBOOK II

青春華語（二）
第二冊 (Beginning Level)

Editorial Board（編輯委員）：

（VC Chinese Team）Dr. Shih-chang Hsin（信世昌）、Dr. Wo-hsin Chu（朱我芯）、Dr. Dolma Ching-wei Wang（王晴薇）、Dr. Chia-ling Hsieh（謝佳玲）

Editor-in-chief主編：Shih-chang Hsin（信世昌）

Executive Editors執行編輯：Huai-xuan Chen（陳懷萱）、Chu-hua Huang（黃琡華）

Consultant編輯顧問：

Dr. Laura Mei-zhi Zhang-Blust（張美智）

Assisstant編輯助理：Yun-jen Lee（李芸蓁）、Run-ting Chang（張閏婷）、Hsiao-ting Huang（黃筱婷）

Graphics插圖：Shi-wen Huang（黃詩雯）

Publisher（發行人）：Rong-chuan Yang（楊榮川）

Chief Editor（總編輯）：Cui-hua Wang（王翠華）

Planning Editor（企劃主編）：Hui-juan Huang（黃惠娟）

Editor（責任編輯）：Chia-ling Tsai（蔡佳伶）

Cover Design（封面設計）：Sheng-wen Huang（黃聖文）

Publisher（出版者）：Wu Nan book publishing Co.（五南圖書出版股份有限公司）

Address（地址）：4th Floor, No. 339, Sec2. Hoping East Road, Da-an District, Taipei 106, Taiwan

　　　　　　（臺灣106 台北市大安區和平東路二段339號4樓）

Phone（電話）：(02)2705-5066　Fax（傳真）：(02)2706-6100

Website（網址）：http://www.wunan.com.tw

E-mail（電子郵件）：wunan@wunan.com.tw

Remittance Account（劃撥帳號）：19628053

Username（戶名）：Wu Nan book publishing Co.（五南圖書出版股份有限公司）

Legal adviser（法律顧問）：Linsheng An LLP Linsheng An attorney

　　　　　　　　　　（林勝安律師事務所　林勝安律師）

* 本教材承蒙國科會數位典藏與數位學習華語文科技與教學國家型科技整合型計畫
【跨國合作之華語遠距協同教學模式研究－美國高中華語課程之設計與實施】
計畫編號：NSC101-2631-S-003-008-、NSC101-2631-S-003-006-）之支持完成，特此感謝。

出版日期：2015年12月初版一刷

定　　價：NT$380（臺幣380元）／US$12